Sister Philomène

Edmond and Jules de Goncourt

Sister Philomène

Translated from the French by
Madeline Jay

Chatto & Windus
LONDON

Published in 1989 by
Chatto & Windus Limited
30 Bedford Square
London WC1B 3SG

A CIP catalogue record for this book is available from the
British Library.

ISBN 0 7011 3277 9

Translation copyright © 1989 Madeline Jay

Typeset by Opus, Oxford

Printed in Great Britain by Mackays of Chatham, Kent.

Introduction

The brothers Goncourt, who were to all intents and purposes one soul and a single writer, were also a prime example of all the ills that can afflict the professional man of letters. Well-born and well-off, they were in the perhaps difficult position of having no obligations, no need for an official position or salary, yet possessed of inordinate ambition. Their ambition was quite simply for recognition, or perhaps more than that, for homage: the literary world was to acknowledge their pre-eminence. That they were distinguished and yet minor writers they could never accept. The fact that they were on fairly intimate terms with all the giants of the day, notably Flaubert, Zola, and Turgenev, bedevilled the position even more; Zola they dismissed, furiously, as their pupil, although there is a world of difference between the great coarse energies and the social indignation of Zola and their own subdued and clinical pity. Mortified in their lifetime, and yet unshakably convinced of their own superiority, they wrote in defiance of the public's appetites, and instead of the long capacious novels to which French literary tastes had been trained by Balzac, they produced miniatures, classic studies of 'cases' which they analysed as if they were doctors, eminent specialists, instead of the seasoned hypochondriacs they never ceased to be.

In one case the hypochondria was not misplaced, since Jules, the younger and more brilliant of the two brothers, died horribly of syphilis in 1870. The account which the elder brother, Edmond,

1

kept of his decline is one of the most painful passages in the chronicles of suffering. Jules' death was followed, in the same year, by the Prussian siege of Paris, which added starvation to the grieving survivor's miseries. Small wonder, then, that the novels written by Edmond alone, after his brother's death, have lost something of that flair and tact that characterise the six novels which they wrote in conjunction before Jules' decline.

The reading public of our own day registers the name Goncourt as the title of a literary prize awarded in France in November of every year. The prize was indeed instituted by Edmond de Goncourt, still mindful of keeping his name forever in the public eye and yet genuinely inspired by a desire to honour the writing profession. His magnificent *Journals* will be known to all who care about the climate of literary Paris in the second half of the nineteenth century. On the strength of these two institutions – the word is not too strong – the name of Goncourt has remained part of the currency of the literary establishment. Yet both Edmond and his brother Jules wished to be remembered as writers, as novelists and playwrights, and the fact that they had only a limited and élitist success, and that their efforts were swamped by the gigantic fame of Zola and the notoriety of Huysmans irritated them profoundly. They could not see why they were not acknowledged as innovators, for they quite rightly perceived that they were writing the sort of novels that no one had attempted before. They claimed that they had invented the working-class novel, yet they did not write with the intention of being read by the working classes. What they did – and it was a fine thing to do – was to write about the poor, in a mood of detached sympathy, in which anger is submerged in pity, so that the plight of the disinherited is examined delicately, painfully, and with unmistakable sadness. Not that they were populist writers: such was not their intention. Rather they saw themselves as applying an altogether superior sensibility to the mute lives on which they trained their considerable intelligence.

They were animated by the great mutual love for each other that sustained them in their isolation from the rest of society, and by their formation as painters, which enabled them to cast an expert eye onto shapes, colours, perspectives. They present the curious phenomenon of a pair who were by nature collectors, bibliophiles, and antiquarians, and yet who became connoisseurs of certain pathological disorders, which they observed, notably, in the uneducated classes. They were also ferocious determinists, and believed that a quirk manifested in childhood, or a path wrongly chosen, would lead inevitably to madness or disgrace. Strong nerves are needed for the dissection of these maladies, yet the brothers were hypersensitive to the point of martyrdom. This makes their procedure as novelists all the more remarkable. Although their tastes led them to salerooms and print shops (Edmond in particular was a notable collector) they manfully descended into the abyss of charity hospitals, working-class funerals, cheap eating houses and dance halls, the studios of unsuccessful painters, the compositors' rooms of popular newspapers, and all the milieux that would enable them to document themselves on their chosen quarry. The six novels written in conjunction by the two brothers before 1870 are therefore characterised by great unfamiliarity: the surprise of seeing these two minor aristocrats dirtying their hands, as it were, in the interests of literature is perhaps unparalleled in the literary annals of the time. This was how they intended it to be.

And yet what survives of their researches exhales an immense sadness. Whether this sadness pertains to their researches, or whether it is inherent in the nature of the brothers Goncourt themselves does not perhaps matter very much; in the best of their novels object and subject merge into a high melancholy. Certainly the lives of those beyond the bourgeois fringe were hard; certainly illness and poverty were starker and more menacing than they have ever been since; but over and above these conditions the reader is aware of a singular and most refined despair. Henry James, reviewing one of the Goncourts' novels, wrote that they signified 'the simple breakdown of joy'. This is true. These novels were not written to entertain or to amuse; they are not conceived as frivolous. Immense discomfort was endured while they were being written and a sort of grief was communicated in the writing itself. Modern readers, coming fresh to the novels of the Goncourts, will not escape a slight sensation of sorrow, as each story delicately, and so expertly, dies on the page.

Modern readers, of course, do not read these novels. Yet there are many reasons why they should. Once they have got over the inevitable distance that separates them from two authors who were always remote, even in their own day, they will find much to beguile them. They should begin with *Soeur Philomène*, first published in Paris in 1861. This story of a nun who is also a nursing sister and whose emotional life has been stifled since her orphan childhood will be perceived as stark in its outline and rigorously simple, yet it is also tender and compassionate in much the same way that Soeur Philomène herself is compassionate, that is to say with a wealth of feeling that has never been allowed its true expression. Everything here is controlled, as reduced in colour as the nun's own garments; the colours actually referred to are all half-tones: off-white, pewter, grey. This severe monochrome suits the story itself, which is dramatic but understated. In other hands it could have been scandalous, a real popular success. But readers should bear in mind that formulation of Henry James: the story is in fact about the simple breakdown of joy, and this is a very subtle matter indeed.

Those on whom the story has its effect might like to go on to read *Renée Mauperin* or *Germinie Lacerteux*, in which the style becomes more elaborate, twisting itself into those frenzies of expression that break out in *Manette Salomon*. The single-name titles indicate the clinical aim: here is a case history to be

4

examined. But the clinical aim is also the writer's aim; it is also the writer's obligation, which is to live his character's life and yet to stand apart. In pursuance of these two functions the Goncourts are exemplary. It is to be hoped that their desire for posterity will be appeased, in however small a degree, by this modern translation of *Soeur Philomène*. It is also to be hoped that its appearance in the England of the 1980s will win more adherents to the small but fervent band of the Goncourts' admirers.

Anita Brookner, London 1988

I

It was a large, lofty hall which stretched out endlessly into deep shadows.

It was night. Two stoves cast a reddish gleam through their open grates. At intervals, nightlights whose small flames dwindled into the distance threw a fiery reflection on the shiny tiles. Their pale, wavering glimmer bleached the curtains against the walls, and revealed rows of beds emerging from the gloom. At the end of the hall, in the dark, a pale outline looked like a plaster virgin.

The air was tepid and moist, with a sickening smell, a syrupy taste of warm ointment and boiled linseed.

All was quiet. No noise, no movement. Night was asleep; silence reigned. But now and then, out of the still shadows, there came a rustling of sheets, a smothered yawn, a timid moan, a sigh . . . Then the heavy, mysterious peace returned.

On a straw-bottomed chair, an oil lamp had been set down next to a little prayerbook; a girl who had been resting both feet on the chair rung, her hair tousled by sleep, got up from a large white-sheeted armchair in which she had been drowsing. Silhouetted against the light, she went to the stove, picked up the poker lying on the hot ashes, stirred the charcoal two or three times, then went back to her seat, placed her feet on the rung again and turned sideways.

The fire glowed redder. In their long glass holders hanging from curved iron supports, the nightlights dimmed, then revived. Their flames rose and fell, as if breathing in and out, over the luminous, transparent oil. The smoke bells swinging over those moving flames threw enormous, ever-shifting circular shadows onto the beams of the ceiling. Below, light flowed softly from the hanging glasses down to the foot of the beds, onto the shirred bands of cloth which framed them, onto the curtains whose shadow it threw like a scarf across bodies curled up under blankets. Shapes and outlines trembled in the shifting half-light and, between the beds, the tall windows, only partly screened by hangings, let in the bluish radiance of a beautiful winter's night, icy and serene.

Between one lamp and the next, outlines wavered and blurred. Outside the patches of light, black shadows rose straight up to the ceiling, bringing night to both sides of the hall. Beyond, the eye could still perceive a vague whiteness; then night returned, a deep night which obliterated everything.

In the deepest shadows, at the end of the ward, a little light wavered, a pinpoint of fire appeared. It came from far away and grew, like a distant glimmer towards which you walk, in the country at night. The light came closer. From behind the large door which separated one ward from the next, it delineated the archway, lit up the glass pane; the door opened: a candle could be seen – then two women, all in white.

'Ah! The Mother doing her rounds,' mumbled a sleepy patient, closing her eyes against the light and turning onto her other side.

The two women in white walked past slowly and quietly. Their steps were so soft that their feet seemed to glide silently across the tiles. They came forward, holding the candle before them, like shadows in a ray of light.

The one on the side of the beds kept her hands crossed in front of her. She was young. Her gentle face had the peaceful smile which dreams sometimes bring to a silent sleeper. She wore the white veil of a novice. Her soft woollen dress, yellow against the cold linen whiteness of the beds, was the white habit of the Sisters of Saint Augustine.

The community maid, in a white vest, white petticoat and night cap, followed in her footsteps. She carried the candle, which lit up her face fully, giving her pasty complexion the cool, chalky look of the head of an old abbess in a dark painting.

As the two women walked past, the light slid over the beds through their open curtains and revealed in passing the open mouth, hollow nostrils and upturned head of a sleeping woman; it flitted across the bony face of a patient whose kerchief was pulled right down to her eyes and whose fist, clenched against her cheek, held the sheet to her mouth; it skipped over the hoop propping up the blankets at the foot of a bed; it showed, moulded by the covers, the pretty shape of a sleeping young woman, her left arm folded like a crown under her hair, pale as a sacrificial host in the shadows.

The sister glanced at the sleeping patients; to those who were awake she gave a little nod, a friendly look, a greeting, a smile, a gentle touch of her hand as she tucked in the sheets and plumped the pillows.

As she walked past, a mumbling voice came from one of the beds, a groan, an angry complaint. The sister went to the head of the bed and took the sick old woman in her arms, lulling her with repeated words, with the sort of sing-song in the coaxing voice used by nannies and mothers to subdue naughty children. She turned her over and leant over her back, her deformed loins, chafed by the bed, marked with red weals like a baby's bottom irritated by its swaddling-clothes. She rocked the old woman's wasted legs, which jerked up, bone against bone, and swiftly drew from under her body the dirty draw-sheet . . . To the soothing words, the gentle touch, the patient only responded with an impatient grumble, an animal moan.

'We'll get you a poultice,' said the sister.

'Don't want it, don't want it,' cried the old woman, in a strangled, muzzy voice.

The sister, with the same gentle words and gestures, settled the patient smoothly, straightened her cap and plumped the flattened pillow around her head.

She continued her rounds. Now and then patients, half sitting up and clinging with one arm to the wooden stick which hung over their beds, and which threw a dancing shadow onto the canopy long after they had released it, stared at her curiously as she went by.

She stopped in front of a screened bed. The four side curtains and the two at the foot were tightly drawn. Their folds fell stiffly to the ground; the two unknotted curtain loops with their two little loosened cords dropped at the corners. Above the closed, veiled bed, on the bare, black metal plate, the hand-written notice which hung over the other beds was missing. The sister went to that bed, lifted one of the curtains and slipped behind it for a few seconds. Then her hand, making the sign of the cross, dropped the curtain, which returned to its motionless folds.

The sister's steps slowed as she approached the door to the maternity ward through which came small cries which were briefly hushed, then started again, lively and stubborn. She listened to the cheerful clamour from the awakening cradles, which sounded to her ears like the gay cheeping of newborn chicks. After the querulous silence of the ward, after all the hushed sounds of sickness, suffering and dying, she felt that those infant wails were life itself . . .

Suddenly, she was called to a bed by a full-throated yell followed by childlike weeping. A bright light shone from within the curtains. A young man stood near the bed, wearing the small skullcap of a houseman and a white apron tied to the top button of his overcoat. With a wax taper held high above his head, he was examining the weeping and moaning patient. The sister drew near.

'No, not you,' he said roughly, taking from her hands the bandage she carried and handing it, with the taper, to the maid who stood on the other side of the bed. His hands moved swiftly over the patient's body as he applied the dressing.

The sister did not answer. She walked away into the darkness of the Saint Theresa ward, and was gone.

II

The sister's religious name was Sister Philomène.

The name on her birth certificate was Marie Gaucher.

She was the daughter of a waistcoat-maker who had married a locksmith and earned about forty sous a day by working for ready-made shops. Marie was born on a bright sunny day during a poverty-stricken January, and was cursed by the charity midwife her birth had disturbed.

She came into life tiny and underweight, with scarcely the strength to live. Her mother fed her with the thin milk of women who work late. In spite of everything, the infant survived. She was four when her mother died.

Her father had left a year earlier, with a workmate who was going to Africa. Nobody knew what had become of him.

The child was adopted by an aunt, her mother's elder sister, who was in the service of a widowed lady, Madame de Viry, in the rue de la Chaussée d'Antin. She had worked there for twenty years. She had closed Monsieur de Viry's eyes; she had attended the birth of their little boy, Henry; she was one of those old retainers who grow roots within the family home. So when, one evening while undressing her mistress, she started talking about her niece, Madame de Viry anticipated her request: on the day of her mother's funeral, the little girl was brought to the rue de la Chaussée d'Antin and settled in. She showed no surprise at entering this new home. She felt no awkwardness, no curiosity about the furniture, the carpets, the mahogany writing desk, the clock with its Greek statuette, the portraits in their gilt frames. And soon she blossomed in that prosperous household. Shy and awkward at first, she became more graceful; she chattered and laughed more freely; her gestures grew bolder and the sickly, awkward child fluttered lightly like a bird. Madame de Viry, who had borne her widowhood like an austere duty and had withdrawn from the world to devote herself entirely to her son, was amused by the child who, through her games, her noise, her flashing blue eyes, filled and warmed her lonely, sometimes sad life. Madame de Viry had herself lost a little girl of that age, and mothers are good at fostering the shadow of a lost child.

The little girl let herself be spoilt and indulged. Tolerated as a pet in the drawing room, she found herself quite at home. When she played with little Henry, she treated him as a companion, in a childish spirit of complete equality. Her aunt was flattered by the small liberties which the child was given and took so sweetly: she was secretly proud to see her behaving like a little lady outside the kitchen. Each of her minor transgressions – her small presumptions, her young vanity swelling as she approached and entered a higher society, her coquettish enjoyment of the presents Madame de Viry made her of her faded ribbons and old frocks – delighted the good woman, who began, quite naturally, to look up to the little girl as better born than herself, and destined for a higher position than her own. Marie was at an age when social barriers, crossed playfully, are invisible; she started deluding herself and putting on airs with her aunt's friends and with the other servants. She treated with a young lady's reserve the coal-merchant's daughters who wanted to play with her on the pavement. Madame de Viry invited her to dinner with Henry, who had won the Cross of Good Behaviour at his boarding school; the next day she refused to eat in the kitchen with her aunt. When she was not allowed to join the children's party which Madame de Viry gave every year on Shrove Tuesday, she sulked for a whole day on a chair in the entrance hall, with tears in her eyes which she concealed and managed to control. She was hurt by a thousand little occurrences which she did not understand, but felt; the slightest omission, a careless word, the trifles through which the world unthinkingly reveals social inequalities, all she instinctively perceived of her inferior position in the house, left her bitterly humiliated. After two years, Madame de Viry understood the child's resentment and pain. For the sake of her own happiness, of her future, she would have to be removed to another environment. With great heartache the aunt accepted Madame de Viry's explanations, without fully understanding them. It was decided between servant and mistress that the little girl would be enrolled the following Monday in a school for poor orphans run by the Sisters of Saint —, at the top of the Faubourg Saint-Denis.

On her last day there was a terrible scene. The little girl, choking with sobs, clung to the furniture, to Madame de Viry's skirts. She struggled with all her strength, even in the arms of her aunt who had to carry her away. As she entered the convent gate, her violent despair abated; her pain became that of a grown-up, silent and icy. When the sisters removed her lace bonnet and her silk frock, made out of her mother's wedding dress which her aunt had dyed, when they put on her head the little ruched linen bonnet and on her body the plain green merino frock, she shuddered slightly; but her reddened eyes remained dry. Once in bed, the tears flooded back. She remained awake until midnight. Through her closed eyes, against a black veil on which flitted moving lights, like sparks racing along burnt paper, she saw outlined, close enough to touch, the drawing room corner where she used to put her doll in disgrace. From the depths of a dark canvas, memories emerged unbidden. Now it was the champagne-bottle basket in which her aunt used to put her at night, before taking her up to her own room on the fifth floor – and the sheet of the cot where she lay in the dormitory seemed to reproduce the folds of the napkins on which she used to lie in that basket; now it was those playful mornings when, returning with her aunt from shopping for lunch, she would jump like a big dog onto Monsieur Henry's bed and put her frozen little hands inside his shirt collar until the sleepy boy, half angry, half laughing, would open one eye and throw her down on the carpet.

As there was already a little girl called Marie in the convent, she was told the next morning that from now on her name would be Philomène. For the child, that was the last deprivation. It had been less of a wrench when her frock had been removed from her body. She felt she had lost all that remained of Madame de Viry's house, of her days of happiness. She hated the name Philomène, which represented for her the frightening baptism of convent life, and for a long time she refused to answer to it.

During the first few days, the sisters spoilt her and tried to amuse her; but she responded to their kissing and fussing with apathy, with dull patience, silent despair. The peaceful, silent house, with its high, bare walls seemed dead to her; she found the sisters stern and frightening even in their gentleness, and she withdrew nervously within herself. The very air she breathed froze her heart, and she kept all her tenderness locked inside, as if to warm herself. She remembered her aunt's kisses, so unlike the sisters' kisses, in which she sensed an impersonal compassion which did not satisfy her. For the first time in her life, she found caresses cold.

And yet, gradually, her anguish was easing. Habit and boredom were wearing down her sorrow, lulled by the even flow of time, by discipline and the unchanging order of tasks, the sameness of one day to the next, by a life devoid of incident, always identical, from morning to night: rising at five; housework, in which all the little girls took part, some making beds, some dragging the bedside rugs down into the yard, shaking them and breathing in the dust; soup at nine; lessons till twelve – writing, reading, scripture, the four rules of arithmetic; dinner at midday, with soup and the inescapable boiled beef which the children called 'scrag'; at one, the bell calling them away from the playground to the needlework which was the convent's livelihood; the workroom, where the youngest hemmed tea-cloths and the cleverest attempted buttonholes; at three, a piece of bread followed by a short break; from them till seven, more needlework, more tea-cloths; then a vegetable supper, playtime and bedtime at nine.

She was no longer seen weeping. She no longer thought of running away; she seemed changed as after an illness. She, who had been so lively, so cheerful and boisterous, no longer chattered or lost her temper. During break, the sisters almost had to force her to play. She became strangely quiet, even slow; her voice developed a drawl, a sort of whine. She had the bearing, the submissive, repressed look, of those poor waifs who seem to drag the winter behind them. The sisters were not displeased with her: she worked without zeal, but without careless mistakes. They could only tax her with laziness.

But the convent atmosphere, and her passive existence, had only outwardly smothered the child's ardent nature. Her thoughts were all the keener in her less active body. She would be in a fever for the whole week which preceded the first Sunday in the month, visiting day, when her aunt came to see her. When the little girl was finally called to the parlour, she reached it so pale and shaking that, several times, her aunt feared she would faint. Then everything she had meant to tell her since the last visit crowded into her soft, broken speech. She would start sentences, trains of thought, and suddenly, not knowing how to say it all, would stop abruptly, looking at her aunt. Then, clinging to the old woman, who laughed and felt like crying, putting both arms around her neck, she would cuddle up to her and push their two heads together; and thus, looking up into her aunt's eyes with each question, she would ask about the house porter, the dairy woman, about Madame de Viry and Monsieur Henry; whether they still talked about her, whether Monsieur Henry still remembered her and when she could write to him for his name-day. At one o'clock sharp they had to part. The parlour door would close, the little one would leave; but then, she would push the door ajar and, peering out with a last sad, teasing smile, blow her aunt a kiss. If her aunt missed the midday visit, the child would feel, between twelve and one, a painful shock, almost a blow to the heart, every time one of her friends was called to the parlour. She kept fidgeting during Vespers. On the bench where she sat with the other girls, in the long row of little white bonnets with transparent tops darkened by the children's hair, among all those motionless heads, her little head kept stirring. At last her eye would find in the church, amidst all the headgear, the blue-ribboned bonnet belonging to her aunt. The old woman was waiting for her at the door and walked her back to the convent: the child wanted to walk abreast with her, arm in arm, next to her classmates.

The church likes to surround children with young and pretty faces. She knows how much young creatures, whose senses awaken their souls, are aware of the looks of those around them. She tries to appeal to their eyes, to win them through the charm of the women who care for them, bring them up, teach them. She chooses among the sisters the most friendly, lively faces to place near the children. She seems to attempt, through the smiles on the faces of those young sisters, to bring back to the little orphans the shadow of their mothers' smiles.

Of the ten sisters who cared for the orphans, almost all were young and pretty. Even those who lacked regular features had a softness in their eyes, a gentleness on their lips, which made them graceful and lovable. Only one among them was quite ugly.

She was almost a hunchback, with one shoulder higher than the other. She spoke with an accent from Gascony, which sounded quite ridiculous in her mouth. Worse still, she had a face like a mask. One could neither see nor hear her without thinking of Mr Punch: the children called her Sister Wicked Fairy. She gestured like a man, crossed her legs, slapped her thighs as she talked; sometimes she held her hands behind her back. Her manner was rough and abrupt and at first sight she was almost frightening, with her finger-thick black eyebrows. But in spite of her appearance, Sister Marguerite was a kind soul. The miserable allowance paid by her family, who belonged to country gentry in Périgord, was all spent on treating her pupils with pastries when they were out on their walks. When she saw, surrounded by her classmates, the sensitive, lonely little girl, with no heart for play, the good sister understood that there was a deep hurt within that child whom the other sisters, finding their first approaches rejected, had left to her solitude. She grew fond of Philomène, looked after her during playtime, bought her a skipping rope, and had her sewing duties reduced as they were too heavy for her. Philomène became her protégée, her adopted orphan. One day, after the small afternoon meal, suddenly, without cause, Philomène threw herself into Sister Marguerite's arms and burst into tears, knowing no other way of thanking her. Speechless, the sister was beginning to cry too, without knowing why, when suddenly the child burst into a peal of laughter which brought a light into her wet eyes; looking up, she had seen a ridiculous sight: Sister Wicked Fairy with tears on her cheeks.

From then on Philomène became like the other little girls in the orphanage. Her face still had its earnest look, but was no longer sulky. She again took an interest in childish things. She recovered the intensity, the appetites, the infatuations, the lively health of youth. She enjoyed games again. Competition excited her. She took an interest in her work. She often thought of the large silver heart of the Virgin Mary, placed against the oratory wall, to which were pinned the names of those of the girls who had obtained the best marks during the week; and she envied all the little distinctions rewarding good behaviour in the workroom, the green ribbon and the silver medal of the Christ Child, the red ribbon of Saint Louis of Gonzaga, the white ribbon of the Holy Angels.

Every week now brought a great treat, the Thursday walk, which had at first seemed so dull to her.

The sisters nearly always led the children along Saint Martin's Canal. The girls walked two by two, trailing behind them a buzzing of whispers, like a beehive, watching on the way a boy fishing, a dog running on a barge, a barrow pushed along a folding plank; enjoying all those sights and noises of Paris.

On Assumption Day, the Mother Superior's name-day and two or three other times a year, they went into the country. Usually they were taken to Saint-Cloud. They set out along the park, then, crossing the Pont de Sèvres, they walked along the river, under the trees, to an inn in Suresnes. There they sat down under the trees, jostling each other, at the wooden tables stained blue with wine, and feasted on a large cream cheese provided by Sister Marguerite.

Philomène, even more than the other girls, treasured those days of joy, freedom, open air, games in the high grass and picking flowers under the willow trees. She would wake up on the following morning full of those impressions and, when the picture of the clouds, the path, the river, had vanished from her mind, she still clung to the memory of the sunshine, the scents, the echo of that landscape which she could no longer see: the smell of the trees, the lapping of water came back to her, as if from afar.

One day above all she remembered. Returning from the country, they visited a market garden near Paris. It was a day in May. The sky was alight with an infinite radiance. It looked as if a quivering gauze had been thrown over a white sky. The air was like a breath of the morning. From time to time, a breeze would rise, sending a shiver through the trees and brushing against the little girls' ears with a fluttering caress. In the peaceful daylight, under that sky and that breeze, the pear trees, peach trees, cherry and apricot trees spread out a silver net of white blossom on every branch. Under the apple trees, over the brown earth, it looked as if somebody had scattered the petals of a bunch of flowers; and the sun, racing through the hearts of the trees, flitted like a bird in the snow. Nature seemed adorned as if for the feast of the Virgin, and the dazzling orchard, seen briefly in its white spring splendour, left in Philomène's soul the inner light, the soft, delightful radiance of a vision.

As the child unconsciously treasured in her memory such sights and sensations, she became more sensitive, more touchy. She grew sad, almost cross, when the sisters were affectionate with the other girls. An unspoken word, a question unasked hurt her like forgetfulness and indifference. She had such a deep need of care, interest, affection, that any kindness lavished on others struck her as stolen from her; and sometimes the fears of which she was ashamed, the sufferings which she concealed, erupted into jealous demands. One day the whole convent spent an afternoon in Madame de Maureuil's manor, near Lagny. Madame de Maureuil was the convent's patron, and every year she offered a memorable afternoon meal to the little orphans. In the evening the carriages brought the children home. They had drunk a few drops of champagne and were all, without listening to each other, remembering aloud, as though in a dream, the beautiful things they had seen: the moats with running water; the large gate with gilded decorations; the avenue where ivy festooned the trees; and the silk-covered furniture; and the large gallery where family portraits stared at them while they were eating; and the park, which seemed endless; and the marble statues; and the flowers in the conservatory, whose names they didn't know and which looked as if they were made of wax. Amidst all the noise, the admiring exclamations, Philomène alone remained cool and said nothing.

'Well then, tight mouth,' said Sister Marguerite, 'have you nothing to say? Perhaps it wasn't beautiful enough for you? What's the matter with you, naughty girl? Come on! I know: you would have liked to be among the big girls . . . to have the lady talk to you . . . I know how you are . . . You are . . .'

The sister stopped abruptly, and heaved an understanding sigh as she looked at the child. That night, before Philomène fell asleep she felt the sheet pulled up over her hands and her uncovered shoulders by Sister Marguerite.

The sister's care and kind attentions did not alienate the child's affections from the Chaussée d'Antin. Her thoughts still dwelt on her memories, still flew to her aunt, to Madame de Viry, to Monsieur Henry. The first Sunday in the month was still the great day in her life. She didn't tremble quite so much when she went down to the parlour, but she still arrived there with caresses for her aunt. When she was grown up, she would go back to Madame de Viry – she always extracted that same promise from the old woman, with an anxious 'Isn't that so?' which came straight from her soul.

Apart from those Sundays, there were three weeks in the year which filled Philomène with deep emotion: the week before the New Year, the week before Madame de Viry's name-day, and the week before her aunt's name-day. During those weeks she was constantly planning her message of congratulations, which she wished to be beautifully expressed. From a girl who had been given stationery, she would buy some pretty notepaper, surrounded with a garland of embossed roses. How she tried, shyly and awkwardly, to work out elegant sentences just like those she had read in books! What care she took to write well, to close her *a*s and not to make any blots! Once the letter was finished, closed with transparent sealing wax, how she calculated so that it would arrive just on the eve of the day!

When Philomène was ten, a girl two years older came to the convent. The two children, on seeing each other for the first time, rushed towards each other with an instinctive impulse. The great friendship at first sight was sealed at playtime the next day by a present which the newcomer, Céline, gave Philomène. For a long time Philomène thought this present was the most beautiful thing in the world. It was an envelope of embossed lacy paper, looking like gauze and outlining a vase on which was written in gold, amidst gilt ornaments, the word *Souvenir*. Out of this envelope one pulled a bunch of lilac, painted and cut out, which fanned out into seven sides on which small engraved medallions in smooth-cut showed the baby Jesus on the straw of his crib, surrounded by kneeling children. Philomène tucked the beautiful picture in her prayerbook; often, during the first few days, she would unfold it, look at the pictures, and read again the litany which ran round the medallions: *Jesus! sweet Saviour, as a New Year's gift, please accept my heart.*

The two girls became close friends. They never left each other's side; they shared all their treats: their sugar, their butter. They shared their thoughts, their joys, their pains. During playtime, they were always seen together. Sometimes the arm of one would be round the other's neck or absent-mindedly round her waist while they chatted; they walked from one end of the playground to the other, linked by some childish gesture, leaning confidentially towards each other: Philomène with her big eyes and long eyelashes, her lingering gaze, her full mouth, her red, slightly suntanned cheeks shaded by the loose curls pouring out of her bonnet; Céline with her rounded forehead, her naturally curly hair, her small, clear, deep grey eyes, her flaring nostrils, her thin lips, her cleft chin, her long thin face. Often, after a few turns, they would sit on the stone bench near the pump. Even in winter they would stay there for a long time, resting the tips of their flopping list slippers on the beaten earth, wrapped up in the printed calico dresses with thin pleats under which one could make out bunched-up, thick knitted waistcoats; they let themselves grow numb with cold, pleasantly lazy, silent and motionless, their eyes turned upwards, Philomène looking at a bird, Céline at a cloud.

Until she came to the convent, Céline had looked after her invalid grandmother. From her early years, she had been brought up on *The Lives of the Saints*. The old woman used to read a few pages to her every night, opening the ancient book with her gouty fingers at the mark left the day before. Then a time came when Céline in her turn took the heavy volume on her lap and read from it to her grandmother. She had learnt to read in that book: her imagination had spelt out the letters and her life started with that first alphabet as an initiation.

All those holy miracles, adventures, sacrifices, heroic deeds, glorious agonies, divine deaths, opening heavens and raining palms had dazzled her with a fairyland of miracles. The stories of *The Golden Legend* filled her head and seemed to swell her forehead, which resembled that of a little Memling Virgin, almost deformed by the bumps of marvel-seeking. An enchanted world rose up from those pages, as delightful as the world of fairy-tales through which nurses give play at the same time to the dreams and the first thoughts of children. She found in those stories of saints and martyrs, full of apparitions, monsters and metamorphoses, the delight, the obsessions, the emotions, the sweet flights of fantasy and the idealised reality which fairy-tales bring to young souls. Since nothing happened in her life with the old woman to upset the child's illusions, since she met around her neither doubt nor smiles which could have disturbed her naïve and passionate impressions, for her, in the first flush of her faith, the path which Tom Thumb scattered with breadcrumbs was the road in the desert planted with rushes every half league by Saint Macarius; the talking bird of Indian tales was the grasshopper calling Saint Gregory; the singing water was the piece of ice asking Saint Theobald for masses for the soul enclosed within. No palace with diamond gates built with a stroke from a fairy rod, within which

Sleeping Beauty had slumbered for a hundred years, arose before her; but she thought of gold ladders resting on the ground, of paths covered with magnificent shining carpets leading a saint's soul from his cell to celestial glory. Her fears, even when she was in bed without a light, were not the usual childish fears: she did not imagine an ogre or a bogey-man or robbers: what darkness outlined with shining embers, what insomnia brought to her was the Devil, as she had seen him in the Legend, ready to tempt a saint.

By daylight, the lands inhabited by saints spread out in front of her in shining, blurred perspectives. She would repeat words which sounded in her ear like a shell from an Eastern sea; and the name of King Gondophares echoed as from a faraway kingdom. Then there were vaults in which, suddenly, the voices of angels silenced human voices ... 'Why are you so silent today?' her grandmother would ask, while the little girl's needle mechanically seamed a napkin or mended a stocking. The child only answered with a smile from her eyes: she was dreaming of solitude, of a desert, a hermitage in a corner of the Monceau plain, beyond Paris, in a place she knew.

As an accompaniment to real life, such ideas, such dreams, had become Céline's soul life. Soon it was not enough for her to share those miraculous stories in thought alone. The long martyrology, constantly showing sacrifices and offerings to God, required her own immolation. She tried to achieve martyrdom silently, in her own way. She mortified as much as possible her innocent little senses. She deprived herself of the dishes she liked. She forced herself to recite a number of *Aves* while walking along a street. She took vows of silence for half a day. When she went to bed with the overwhelming sleepiness of childhood, she forced herself to remain awake for several hours, until a time she had chosen. Sometimes, when her grandmother offered her a walk or a treat, she punished herself by pretending she was sick and going to bed.

Church-going, confession and her first communion had fed the ardour of her mystic temperament. Céline had refined those little sacrifices, and by ingeniously sharpening and intensifying their deprivations, she had carried them almost to the point of cruelty. She felt some pride in testing her sickly body, which was frail, but which already had a strong resistance to pain. She had always been greatly attracted by the tales of young Christian women, tortured in front of the Proconsul, whose limbs, torn by iron prongs, poured out milk from their wounds instead of blood.

More delicate, more sensitive, less dreamy though more tender than her friend, Philomène was gently teased and lectured by Céline. With a proselytising zeal which already inspired and refined her relationships, Céline had taken it upon herself to support, to rouse, to improve a soul which she saw as lazy and weak. Using persuasion and advice, the influence of her serious talk, the lesson of her example, she gradually dragged her companion out of the indolence of her age and nature. She encouraged her along the path of small sacrifices, not without difficulty and much patience. She had to gain ground step by step, always returning the next day to what she had won the day before, always struggling with reason, irony without bitterness, prayers, emotional pleadings, against Philomène's doubts, her timid defences, the resistance and excuses of her tepid will. Philomène often complained that she had not enough strength, that too much was expected of her. But Céline was never at a loss for answers. She always had, as a final argument, some model to put forward, the virtue of a saint which should be emulated. And she countered the moaning from her friend's soul as well as the groaning from her body; for instance, when Philomène was disgusted by the boiled meat which formed part of all their dinners: 'Ah, my dear, do think of Saint Angela . . . Three walnuts, three chestnuts, three figs, three leeks, that was all she ate . . . and bread only on Sundays . . . and *you* complain!'

Souls like Philomène's are soft and pliable. She was easily influenced by Céline's enthusiasm. During playtime, when their little scatterbrained classmates sang around her:

> I love wine
> I love brie!
> I love Susie!

She retorted with Céline:

> I love the convent!
> I love the convent!
> I love the convent!

Her friend's faith became her own; but her temperament gave it a personal bent and expression. What was for Céline a contained, concentrated fire was for her a spreading flame: her exaltation made her grow.

The sisters were delighted with this surprising change; they saw a divine grace in the transformation of a child they had known until then as absent-minded and negligent in her faith, and whom they now used as an example of piety, regularity, and punctuality to the other girls.

Every day, on waking up, Philomène made the sign of the cross and offered her first thought to God. While dressing, she asked for the cloak of innocence which she had lost through sin. Before starting work, she laid her tasks at the Lord's feet to expiate her faults. She never forgot to say a little prayer on the hour. At nine she thought, while praying, of the Holy Ghost who had descended over the Apostles on the day of Pentecost at that time; at midday, she appealed to the angel Gabriel. Before dinner, a short personal examination of her faults lasted the time of a *Miserere*. Before playtime, she asked God to guard her lips. At the time when Christ surrendered His spirit to His father, she prayed to Jesus to tie her to His cross so she would never come down from it. At night, while praying before going to bed, she never failed to kiss the ground three times. If she woke up during the night, she joined in thought the servants who praise the name of the Lord in the night, the worship of blessed spirits, the anthems of saints in Paradise. Then she tried to go back to sleep in a bodily position which showed respect for God's eye and which she would have wanted for herself if death had taken her by surprise, unprepared as she was.

Her first communion occurred in the middle of that pious phase which was due to Céline. It was a great event for the little girl. Lengthily prepared by the Saturday catechism class, she was stirred in advance by the excitement of the great day. The week before that beautiful and awesome Sunday, the retreat, with its continuous exercises, instructions, exhortations, inflamed her zeal. Cut off from life and outside thoughts, meditating during long vigils, constantly invoking the flesh and blood of Jesus Christ, Philomène was thrown into a sort of ecstasy by the delightful mystery of a union with God through her lips. Abstinence, fasting, and her weakened body, ill supported in its development by the meagre convent fare, helped the detachment of her senses, the heightening of her whole being. Through the spiritual exaltation and the nervous excitement of ceaseless praying, of a worship now whipped up by enthusiasm, now softened by contrition, she felt her soul, softly carried away, escaping from her body. All her blood seemed to rush to her head and to her heart. She was shaken by secret tremors, inner shivers and all the reactions of her childish imagination mixing with God and touching him lovingly. She came out of confession with her face bathed in tears which she happily allowed to run down her cheeks and to moisten her lips. It was a passionate longing for her first approach to the holy table, with all the stirrings, the unknown fever, the new sensations, the intimate revelations which it brings to a twelve-year-old girl. She thought she was called from above, she was waking up to a new

26

awareness of herself as if she had broken with one stage of her life suddenly to enter another, as if her childish soul was being transformed by the first moral feelings of womanhood.

At last, the divine communion day arrived. Philomène had asked her aunt to bring her some eau-de-Cologne for her handkerchief and scented pomatum for her hair. Entering the church among the communicants, she felt stunned, unable to see or hear anything. She was so moved that she had neither command nor awareness of her own movements. There was a loud humming sound inside and around her; she let herself be enfolded by the scents she wore as by a breath from heaven, without knowing where they came from. Sunbeams were playing around the church, casting over the altar rubies from the stained windows. Blue smoke was rising in the dusty light. The burning candles shone like stars among the white dresses. Voices rose among the scents, prayers rose with the songs. Censers were shaken with a muffled noise by white-gloved hands . . . But for Philomène, the whole church was the altar; the whole altar was the tabernacle. She kept her eyes on it; she yearned for it and strained to fasten her inner vision to it. Concentrating her glance and her mind, trying to see through the cloud which sight casts around things after a while, she saw, behind the piece of gilt wood, only what one sees of the sun behind a hill which hides the dawn.

Her row stood up: she stood up. Her turn came, she received God. While receiving Him, she had an inexpressible feeling of weakness, the ecstasy of a sort of fainting.

The church now became for Philomène a holy place, intimate and tender like a room where you were born and where you have loved your mother. She waited for Sundays when she could go there, live there for a whole day, from Holy Mass to the advanced catechism class, and from Vespers to Compline.

And yet Saint-Laurent, where the sisters took the children, was but a poor church. Looming at the top of the boulevard de

Strasbourg, it looked like one of those forgotten old provincial churches on a lonely square where a rope-maker spins out his rope. Inside, it was cold and bare: you were in the poverty-stricken parish of the faubourgs Saint-Denis and Saint-Martin. Under its stiff vault, along its dirty grey walls, you could hear dragging steps, slithering boots on the flagstones, a hollow winter cough. The faithful consisted of a second-hand clothes dealer with a handkerchief over her head, a servant carrying the dinner of her small household in a napkin, a coal-merchant's wife hissing a silent prayer between her lips, a mother with a shopping bag and a very small child in her arms, over whom she made the sign of the cross as she came in, a little working girl with bowed head, praying and holding her mouth between fingers blackened by needle marks. There were women in mourning wearing old gowns and old black hats with veils turning russet. Against the chapel railings, you could often see some old woman in a linen cap, with a fixed stare, her eyes turned up with dilated whites and mumbling lips. Sometimes in a corner, a bent old man in a faded blue overcoat over his shoulders was kneeling on the ground.

But Philomène saw none of these sad sights. She did not notice that the church was shabby, because she was happy there. She attributed her happiness to the place and to her surroundings. She felt a vague well-being, an infinite peace, a dreamy laziness, a languid fulfilment. The charm to which she surrendered on her bench in the nave was like a softness in the air, like the enervating effect of a warm climate; when she breathed that cool, subtle church air, she felt bathed in the atmosphere of an ideal homeland.

She loved, as she went in, the cold feel at her fingertips of the holy-water sprinkler with its frosted bristles. She loved the vapours of burning wax, the smell of cold incense, the fading scents of balsam and candles which filled the church with a fragrance of dried flowers as the smoke melted away. She enjoyed the peace with its mysterious noises: a muffled step, a fluttering skirt, a turning page, the kneeling of silent prayer, the muttering of praying lips, the silent elevation of the Host, like a whisper of souls. She was lulled by the sound of the organ, by melodies which carried her away like a flowing stream, by clusters of sound, tempests of noise which gathered and rolled over her, by celestial choirs which sang in her head and hummed inside her chest, angel anthems which came down and died slowly within her. She listened, delighted, to the songs of priests and children, answered from the depths of chapels by faraway voices, young and old. And she was deliciously stirred, during Vespers, by the voice of a singer, uplifted, thin and high; a falsetto voice which seemed to rise to God on an echo of the Passion.

The voices, the music, the atmosphere and scents of the church affected her more sweetly as the day wore on. Her thoughts wavered lazily in the half-light which bleached the windows, threw a snowy reflection over the top of the confessional boxes and vaguely mixed its faint whiteness with the pink gleam of the candles and lamps reflected under the vaults. She was half asleep, surrendering with a secret delight to the dreams and shadows of the dying day, letting her glance wander over the depths of the dimmed chapels, over dark corners around the choir where a white cap, a colourless face, a black shawl or the white edging of a bunched-up petticoat suggested without revealing them ghostly women lined up on a bench. And when, at the end of the last service, the scraping of chairs jolted her out of her numbness, she emerged like a sleeper suddenly awakened from a dream.

The church was to become even dearer to her. There was, behind the choir, in the chevet, a chapel towards which went all the poor people who entered. In front, in the dark recess of an angle of the wall, over four rows of long forks resting on a wooden stand, thin little candles were burning, sending quivers through the surrounding gloom with their uneven, jumpy tallow flames. By their weak light, one could make out a shadow against the wooden stand, an exhausted, prostrate body, doubled up like Christ in a Deposition from the Cross: a creature smothered in a hooded cloak out of which a hand stuck out to receive two sous for each candle. The chapel entrance was next. On a white and gold altar covered with a lace cloth over faded blue silk, going green with age, amidst artificial flowers under globes with rosewood legs, rose a white Virgin bearing on her chest seven burning golden hearts hanging from a ribbon of white moire: the Virgin of the Seven Sorrows emerging from an azure background striped with golden beams issuing from a triangle. Smiling sweetly, like a twenty-year-old queen, she gracefully supported over a large globe a baby Jesus with a necklace of chaplets and medals, who seemed to think only of playing with the little Saint John. At the top of the altar, on a carved pediment, one could read, in large blue letters on simulated green marble: *Guild of the blessed and immaculate Mother of God, Our Lady of the Sick. Privileged Altar.*

Madame de Viry had contracted the illness which was to kill her after a long year of suffering. Philomène was granted leave from the sisters to go and pray every Sunday in that chapel of 'Supplications for the Sick'. She stood at the entrance against the wall covered with white marble plaques, next to the gilt inscriptions which filled the wall with grateful cries such as: *To Mary, 20th April 18. – I prayed to Mary and she heard me. – O Mary! O my Mother!* She remained kneeling for a long hour; among those women, mothers, daughters, wives, sisters of the sick, praying to the Virgin as if to hope itself. She could be recognised by her deep kneeling, her bowed head, her rounded back, her shoulders raised by the leaning of her elbows on the flat top of her chair, her skirt whose straight folds, falling from her waist to the ground, broke upon her protruding heels.

Philomène's health had deteriorated recently. Her complexion, once bright like that of a child at play, the colour of her pretty little cheeks, were fading. The red of her lips seemed to blanch and turn the shade of violets. She was quite pale. Her hands, no longer reddened, were thinning. A general malaise, pains which moved around every day, continually gave her an uncomfortable awareness of all parts of her body, a feeling of the laborious work of her organs, of the struggle of all her living being. She woke up tired, oppressed by an overwhelming weakness. Climbing stairs or running gave her palpitations: she had to sit down. The slightest work required a great effort of will, a victory over herself. She allowed herself to slip into a sleepiness which lulled her throughts and her senses. Vague ideas of death flitted through her head and her soul. She talked to her aunt about Madame de Viry. She remembered two of her young friends who had died at the age she had now reached. She did not think of dying, but about what follows death, what she would leave behind, to whom she would will her prayerbook, her pictures, her confirmation medal. When she read the mass, her fingers automatically found the mass for the dead: there were Latin words which attracted her in that mass, with a deep, muffled sound which she spelt out. She did not summon these thoughts; she just let herself slide towards them, she surrendered to them as to a fit of dizziness. Nothing, in those ideas, had for her the horror they have for old people, rooted in life and unable to tear themselves away from it. Philomène looked at death calmly, without fear, almost casually. She did not call for it, but she did not repel it either. She was, in a way, quite used to it, and would have greeted it with the feeling of detachment and indifference to life which is sometimes found in young girls at the time of their becoming women.

Her faith grew more intense with such thoughts, more passionate, more ecstatic. She fed on all the words with which the church invokes the sight of death and nothingness. She dwelt, with a bitter joy, upon those images, those grieving words scattered throughout devotional books like black crosses in a churchyard.

But while her faith was keener, her temper was no longer even. Philomène, once so sweet, had become irritable, impatient. She had fits of anger, even against Céline, and would burst into tears when her friend asked her why she was cross with her. Sometimes she could not help weeping. The sisters no longer found her respectful as she used to be, no longer cheerfully ready to do what she was told. She was now reluctant to do the washing up, to help with the cooking or housework as everyone did in turn; and that reluctance was expressed by bad temper and sulking. She had changed, she was disorderly, unlike herself. She had strange food fads: for two months she pestered her aunt to bring her a jar of mustard, which the old woman kept forgetting.

Then her eyes troubled her; she suffered from a sty which soon turned into ophthalmia. The sister in charge of the dispensary, where medicines were provided for the poor, nursed Philomène, but unguents did not help, the ailment worsened. It was decided to send Philomène to the free surgery which Monsieur Nélaton held every Thursday at the medical school. As it would have been a wasted day for the teaching sister or the sister in charge of the sewing class, her aunt was asked to look after her on that day. The aunt came an hour before the time Philomène expected her: she wanted to take her niece to lunch at home, and show Monsieur Henry how much she had grown.

On the way, Philomène hardly talked to her aunt, she was in such a hurry to get there. She walked ahead, her small feverish steps outpacing the weary steps of the old woman who was trying to catch up. At last they reached the street, then the staircase, then the door of the new apartment rented by Monsieur Henry since his mother's death. The door opened and Philomène rushed in behind her aunt. She wanted to see everything, to inspect everything: this was new, that dated from her time and she remembered it; she went from one thing to another, touching the mementoes of her childhood or marvelling at what was unknown and strange to her in the elegant furniture of a fashionable young man. Her heart was beating hard when, clinging to her aunt's skirts with childish shyness, she entered Monsieur Henry's bedroom.

Monsieur Henry, wearing a blue jacket with red silk braid and matching trousers, was standing in front of a mirror resting against the window hasp: he was shaving with the proud and busy look of a twenty-year-old boy who has grown a beard for the third time and feels a man.

'Ah! it's your little one,' he said, as he lifted up his head to shave under his chin. 'My beard is so tough . . .' and turning round, half-shaven, holding up his horn-handled razor: 'Oh! I wouldn't have recognised you . . . you're a big girl now. Well, are you pleased to be out? To spend a day with your aunt? Ah! yes, of course, your eyes are sore. But that's nothing. You mustn't touch them.' And turning to the aunt, 'I hope you'll give her a good lunch. Ah! Look here! Give me my patent leather boots, I'm going out.'

When Philomène returned to the convent at four o'clock that evening, she was left in the parlour for a few minutes while her aunt explained to the sister the oculist's prescription and the treatment to apply. It had been a grey day and night was falling: a cold light bleached the curtains on the window, threw dull shapeless reflections on the chocolate-brown walls, on the tiling broken up by parents' heavy boots, on the smooth wooden chairs, on the straw-bottomed armchair of the supervising sister, on the large walnut wardrobe where they stored the linen which was brought in from outside for the little boarders to hem or embroider. Nothing had changed in the room, everything was in its usual place, and yet nothing seemed familiar any more to the child. She saw with changed eyes the two lithographs of the Mother Superior in their black painted wooden frames, the soapstone Virgin on the mantelpiece, the china vases with the gilt inscription *Mary* in which stood bunches of hawthorn made of yellowing paper. She wondered why the room and all those things no longer appealed to her. In that room which she was absent-mindedly observing, and which she saw for the first time as cold and bare, she suddenly felt faint with a feeling of anguished loneliness, as on her first day in the convent.

Céline, who was awaiting her return, embraced her with a thousand questions about the doctor, what he had said, what he had prescribed. Philomène answered hurriedly in a few words, then went on talking about the pretty apartment where she had been, about her aunt's kitchen from which one could see trees, about the little room where her aunt had told her she would work when she left the convent. And all the beautiful, rich, strange, fascinating things she had seen were recalled and gushed out in words full of emotion and laughter. It was a wild outpouring, interrupted now and then for an endearment, a kiss, rushing from picture to picture, story to story, from the ruched bonnet her aunt had made her try on to the soap suds Monsieur Henry had left on her cheek when he kissed her. In the end, Philomène noticed that Céline was silent and did not join in her happiness.

'Philomène,' said Céline with sweet seriousness, 'when we are in bed tonight, we shall withdraw in spirit for an hour in Jesus Christ's tomb: we shall ask Him for the love of contemplation and retreat.'

From that time on, Philomène underwent an increase of faith and fervour. Giving all the time she could to prayer, she prolonged its uplifting and inner resonance by keeping, while she worked, its whisper on her lips and its thought within her thoughts. During playtime, she read religious texts. She went to confession and communion whenever she was allowed. During mass and Vespers at Saint-Laurent, she concentrated to exclude any distraction and to give herself entirely to God.

This impulse lasted nearly two years. Then it seemed as if an unknown force invaded her, which she could not resist and which would overwhelm her. Her peace, and even her will, were destroyed through worries and fears which she did not know how to fight. When she wanted to reach God, she no longer found the straight path, the gentle incline which used to take her to Him effortlessly. The divine presence was to her only a thought now, no longer a feeling. All the spiritual foods which had sustained her until then also lost for her their strengthening sweetness. Her faith no longer offered delights and failed to dispel the bitterness, melancholia, displeasure, impatience and worrying disturbances which agitated her conscience. She felt temptations around her; and those temptations which, before, would hardly have needed the effort of a thought to repulse them, now preoccupied her like a fixed idea: she feared them so much that she was obsessed by them. At the same time, amidst that cooling and weakening, her helpless soul was tormented by the idea of a perfection she could not reach but to which she aspired, as in a fever, through all sorts of desires, resolutions, vows and penances. Then, exhausted after embracing that ideal of sainthood, she would become agitated again. Rebellion rose up within her against mortifications; her obedience was no longer willing; her imagination was a torment; and what was left of her will had lost the support of grace.

Thus struggled and withered a soul which had known a complete communion with God, a complete surrender to Him. Every day something died in her, some enthusiasm was stifled; every day increased the deadly sickness of the faith which the Church calls a *drought*, comparing the afflicted soul to soil deprived of water. The more she tried to fight the disease, the more she tried to be cured, the more she strove towards an ideal of perfection which she had not sought when she was healthy and at peace, the more she suffered, the more she found strife and anguish within herself. Only religious doubt could put an end to the struggle in which the poor child was tearing herself apart, and Philomène did not doubt yet. But she prayed and was not comforted.

Why did the things which used to move her now leave her cold? Sadly, she would pick up her prayerbook, a modest volume covered in basan, framed with a thin gold thread and with a marbled blue edge, like all the books from the printing presses of Adrien Leclerc, printer of our Holy Father the Pope and of the Archbishop of Paris. To protect it, she had covered it with a black cloth which she had sewn and quilted herself and which fastened with two dark mother-of-pearl buttons. Between that cloth and the hard cover, she had enclosed all the papers relating to her aunt and to Madame de Viry, and the few letters she had received. The book, whose faded edge had been rubbed the colour of old moss, was thickened by her slipping between the pages holy images, prayers to the dying heart of Jesus and a few flowers gathered during walks which marked a date for her. It was the book of her first communion, of her memories, of her hopes; she had long loved it as a relic and as a friend. Now she opened it and leafed through it: she saw only what can be found in any book: lines and letters. She closed it: it was a dead thing.

Céline saw Philomène's struggles. She tried to help her, to soothe her. She would have liked to share with her the strength of her own will, of her resolution, of her steady faith, of her own vocation which grew more assured, more settled with time. But Philomène, slightly ashamed of herself, repulsed her. Finally, she asked Céline to leave her alone, and drew away from her. Céline, then, would hand her a little note every night after supper, asking her to kiss her when they met on the way to the dormitory; to accompany that kiss, in which she wished to carry Philomène's soul to God, she would usually slip into her friend's hand a small folded paper, carefully framed with a ruler, on which she had inscribed in her finest writing: *Gift of faith which makes God's service sweet and pleasant*; or *Fruit of charity which unites us to God through love*. When Philomène grew colder under that nightly kiss and seemed to hold out her cheek only out of habit,

Céline, instead of those little notes, gave her long letters scribbled surreptitiously in pencil. 'God has put in my heart a love according to Him . . . I shall endeavour to do for you what I believe God wants: for He orders us not only to love Him, but to make Him loved . . . I hope that, if you pray to Mary, she will accept you among her children: and then we shall try, through our good example, to awaken in the hearts of our companions the desire to belong to our family . . . Be more pious and I shall consider it my duty to pray for you to the God of the strong . . .' – such were the sentences and the tone of those letters which Céline always signed: *She who wants to be your companion in the holy hearts of Jesus and Mary.* This went on until Philomène, grown weary, pushed away with an impatient, almost angry gesture, the pencilled paper held out by Céline.

Philomène had found some entertainment, some relief in new ideas to which she surrendered. Thoughts of marriage had come to her, not present as a temptation, or precise as a plan, but blurred, vague, veiled by the softness of things seen from afar. She did not think of anybody in particular she would have liked to marry, she did not know what marriage was; she was simply carried by an instinct without sexual undertones, by a desire without impatience, towards the thought of what it might be. In her imagination arose the pure, white image of a wedding seen through little girls' eyes: a white dress and a crown of orange blossom. Then, sometimes, she dreamt further, of greater sweetness in a community of souls, a life shared by two, devotion, mysterious joys which she did not know, which she could not have named, but which would rise on the horizon of that life.

She still had the innocence of a child, the vocabulary of an angel; no knowledge had yet touched her. She made naïve remarks which no longer belonged to her age and hardly to her sex. One day she was among a group of friends, of whom the oldest was younger than herself. One of them said:

'Have you seen how Berthe blushed, last Sunday, when she saw her cousin in the parlour? Surely she's got a crush on him.'

'Don't be silly!' another said. 'It doesn't make you blush: you grow pale.'

'Really?' said Philomène. 'I thought you only grew pale if you hurt yourself.'

Two great gaps suddenly opened up in Philomène's life: Sister Marguerite was allowed to spend a few months in the South for her health, and Céline left the house to begin her novitiate at the parent establishment of the Sisters of Saint Augustine.

Then Philomène felt smothered by the convent. Her lonely life became unbearable. She longed madly, furiously, obsessively, to leave, to go to her aunt. Time, the walls, even the sky above the playground, everything weighed down on her. Boredom was gnawing into her body as well as into her soul; she was losing her health. The sisters grew worried, they allowed her aunt to visit her more often. The daily convent fare, which seemed to disgust Philomène and which she hardly ate, was replaced by more delicate food. But Philomène grew still paler and thinner; her eyes were feverish in her little worn-out face.

Finally, after six months, during one of her aunt's visits, she threw her arms around the old woman's neck and, covering her with kisses and tears, begged her to take her away, telling her that she was bored to death, that she could stay no longer, that she thought she was going to be ill. The aunt needed all her courage to tell her it was impossible, she was too young. She promised to take her out when she was twenty. By then Monsieur Henry would probably be married, she would be his wife's chambermaid. A last silent tear trickled down Philomène's cheek.

By the end of the week, the aunt received a letter in which Philomène told her that she was sorry about the scene she had made and that she had waited a few days to see if her good intentions were lasting. She ended by saying: ' . . . I hope that, with the grace of God and the advice of our good Mother Superior, it won't happen again. I shall leave this house only by the will of God and yours. Perhaps I shall leave it only to enter . . . I won't finish, time will tell.' The aunt did not understand the last sentence, and was reassured. But the sisters' concern had been awakened by the death, not yet forgotten, of two or three young girls who had succumbed to a decline similar to Philomène's. They noticed that Philomène ate nothing at all in the refectory: they even caught her hiding in her sleeve the bread she was given. The convent doctor was summoned and stated, after examining Philomène, that she was suffering from a stomach disorder. The sisters, deeply frightened, fetched the aunt: after hearing the doctor's pronouncement, she took Philomène away in a cab.

Monsieur Henry was away, travelling in Italy. The aunt had ample time to tend to her niece, to take her for walks and entertain her during her convalescence. Showing the poor child a future which they would share, telling her how much she would need her in her old age, she slowly, gently, revived that crushed heart, that soul already grown weary.

One morning there was a loud ring at the door. Monsieur Henry was back.

'Hullo, old girl, are you all right?' said the young man. 'Ah! here's your niece . . . How dare you be so pale? I say, your aunt told me you're a real church mouse.' He burst out laughing and kissed her on both cheeks. Philomène's whole body was trembling.

'Give me some matches. You must look after yourself,' Monsieur Henry continued, puffing at a cigar, 'and not tire yourself too much. Get my things ready, old girl, so I can go and walk on the boulevards again. Any letter from the rue des Martyrs? By the way, I brought you something, Philomène . . . a rosary, a genuine one, from Rome. It's somewhere in my trunk. Ah, another thing; I'm going to entrust you with a special mission in the house: you must check that no buttons are missing from my shirts.'

With that, Monsieur Henry went out, not to return until the next day.

Serving Monsieur Henry became the main occupation of Philomène's time and thoughts. She surrounded the young man with thousands of small attentions, she surprised him with tiny services. She tried to guess the habits which suited him, the comforts he enjoyed. Monsieur Henry's gloves never lacked a single stitch; his pipes were always cleaned; the slightest details of his appearance were cared for as if the eye and the needle of a provincial mother had supervised them. All the knick-knacks in his bedroom, whose disorder the old aunt had respected, were now marvellously organised, tidy and ready to hand. Monsieur Henry seemed delighted to be so well served, but he hardly thanked Philomène, except for an absent-minded good morning or a rough, friendly word. During lunch, while Philomène served him, he was absorbed by his newspaper, which he rested against his glass, and he hardly said thank you. After lunch, he smoked three pipes without uttering a word, picked up his hat and was not seen for the rest of the day.

That bachelor household, which gave little work to the aunt and niece, left all their evenings free. When winter came, to keep herself awake, the aunt made a habit of walking down to the porter's lodge where the servants from the house took turns at offering tea. There was the porter, a little man toying primly with his eyeglasses. A prosperous widower, he was interested in industrial assets and clever at increasing his small capital through investments and underhand loans. Also a boy with the complexion of brown bread and lips as red as a fresh wound – the groom of the stockbroker on the first floor who, egged on by his master, tried with his raucous voice to imitate the vulgar tone of vaudeville servants. Then, the cook of the lady on the second floor, a foreign lady who was said to spy for Russian diplomats; a large Flemish cook, slightly inebriated with brandy, oozing fat, bursting with laughter and lewd jokes. Often, the cook would bring her husband, the most revolting type of coachman from the Luxembourg gardens, whose nose and forehead seemed to drip alcohol at all times of day and whose chin, gnawed away by a sort of leprosy, was half hidden by a dirty scarf. Two or three maids of kept women, with lizard faces, unfastened bonnets and crude vocabularies, completed the population of the lodge, where could also be found a paralytic's attendant on whose red nose trembled a black wart.

When the lodge was full, it was a most unpleasant gathering. Those men and women reeked of yesterday's wine, of corruption, envy, laziness and all the vices of those in service. Their appetites and their instincts seemed soaked in stable dung, greasy washing-up water and bedroom slops. The vices they had picked up from their masters' tables had gone sour inside them, like the remains of a feast rotting in the pantry. Their conversation consisted of swear-words, informing, malicious gossip and impudent schemes for plundering and cooking the books. There was also the loud laughter of the big Flemish woman, the groom's vulgar jokes, the slang of the kept women's maids and the horrible sickroom stories of the paralytic's nurse. Those sniggering voices made you shiver: they sounded like a gang of convicts on the spree.

A depth of stupidity which Paris had not altered saved the aunt from any feeling of horror or disgust. She laughed like the others and with them, but her faithfulness, her native honesty, her scorn for money allowed her to be unaffected by what she heard and to live amidst such immorality not only without being tempted, but almost without being aware of it. As for Philomène, although she was surprised and frightened at first, troubled by an instinctive disgust, her ignorance hid from her the worst of that world. There were many things she did not understand, words with double meanings which eluded her, obscene gestures which meant nothing to her, shameless avowals to which she attached no more importance than to fables of robbers. In any case, for a while they showed some respect for her candour, her honesty, her innocent youth. In her presence, cynical words were modestly veiled. And everybody in the lodge courted the niece of Monsieur Henry's housekeeper with polite attentions. The groom, who always heard his master talk about a practical approach to life, had summed up the situation from the first day. When he saw the girl, he realised that the aunt was a faithful old retainer looking after a bachelor household. He would marry the niece, join Monsieur Henry's establishment with a philosophical attitude to his wife's honour, settle in, replace, one day, the aunt, who was mortal, and with time become the real ruler in that household where there was nothing to do and where the master was known to be easy-going. Such was immediately his plan. He started courting Philomène by offering her faded bunches of violets and paying her brutal compliments which struck her like blows. From the first, the groom's attentions filled Philomène with an insuperable disgust, and opened her eyes. She suddenly saw the man and his world. She recoiled when he tried to kiss her. But as she was too shy to show her feelings clearly, the people in the lodge attributed her coldness towards the groom to the whims of a little girl straight out of the convent.

Her aunt noticed nothing, and still dragged her to those gatherings. One evening, the groom had been offered a box at the Gaïté Theatre by his employer's mistress, who was acting there, and he invited the aunt and niece. Philomène had to spend four hours knee against knee with the groom, who grew bold in the dark at the back of the box, whilst every now and then the Flemish woman, drunk with excitement, shouted at her: 'Are you enjoying it, then, girlie?' Philomène wished she could have fainted.

She still served Monsieur Henry's lunch every day. Monsieur Henry still read his newspaper while eating. Philomène waited for one word, one request: she would have been content with the absent-minded pat he gave her aunt's old cat without looking at it. She would have liked to devote herself, to sacrifice herself for this young man, the thought of whom had kept, in her girlish imagination, the magic and the overpowering charm of a childhood dream. If he had been ill, she would have spent nights nursing him; if he had lost his fortune, she would have served him for nothing. She imagined all sorts of hardships, of catastrophes, which would have allowed her to give back to that family what they had given her, to pour out her heart. The request for a plate or a silver knife to peel a pear would startle her painfully out of those daydreams in which she indulged, almost wishing for those hardships, those catastrophes to happen. Some days she would have liked Monsieur Henry to scold her, to find fault with her, to show some displeasure: at least then she would have existed for him.

The young girl suffered in secret from the coarseness of the people around her and from her young master's indifference. She was under a constant strain; the very air she breathed brought her nothing but oppression or emptiness. Only her mind had remained in harmony with her social class and expectations; all her other faculties had been heightened by the convent. Religious education had refined her soul's tastes, and through its spiritual essence had carried her so far from the instincts and morality of her equals that Philomène felt, in that world to which she belonged, constraint and the vague feeling of being in exile. Life, which she now touched in all its crudeness, wounded all her senses and she could not get used to those wounds. The earthy passions, the brutal words and actions which are natural to workmen or servants, estranged her from the men whom she feared and despised at the same time. The women were no closer to her, and she did not feel as if she belonged to the same sex as these creatures who, outwardly, showed a completely different nature to hers and seemed to have another kind of femininity. Often, in that low company, eager desires arose in her. She was attracted by a certain elegance, a certain gentleness, a certain respectable behaviour which she could not have defined but which she missed as if she had once lived in high society, with well-bred people. She suffered less from the ignorance, the dishonesty, the unkindness of the other servants than from the way in which that ignorance, that dishonesty, that unkindness manifested themselves. Cynicism, which was new to her, hurt her almost physically. And the young girl who could just read and write, who had no natural wit, whose head had been filled with a few pious books and a few innocent novels, who was less intelligent than most of those men and women, saw herself in their company as a soul in purgatory, because she suffered so much in her instincts and in her feelings.

Her need for tenderness was as unfulfilled as her delicate tastes. The convent and religious life had not only refined her soul, they had also ripened her heart; her awakening sensuality had been mortified by discipline and had turned into a fervent need for love. Born with a tender heart, she had been affected by the voluptuous stirrings of pious books with their ever-repeated images of perfumes and flowers, spring dew, celestial scents, fragrant lilies and musk-roses. She had been moved in the chapel and in the church by the whisper of prayers as sweet as mystic kisses, by the deep, penetrating voice of the father confessor, by the bleeding heart of Jesus which the sisters told her to wear in thought like a nosegay on her chest. She had brought to confession a keenly painful heart, to communion a keenly loving heart. Everything cried out to her: Love! Love! And under the fierce glow of that word which she found everywhere, kneeling in front of Jesus, her soul's spouse, the king of her love, the beloved of her heart, looking up to divine love, sweeter than honey, she had allowed her heart to fill with tenderness and to faint in the love fever in which Correggio and Saint Francis of Sales saw the Virgin die. Such was the heart the young girl had brought from the convent: she felt it burst with anguish inside her.

Philomène had resolved to live with her pain. She showed nothing of it; she kept it in check like an injured man holding and stemming his wound with his hand. In whom could she have confided? Her aunt would not have understood. And to admit her pain would have been to desecrate it.

One night as she was going to bed, Monsieur Henry, who hardly ever returned home before morning, came in. He was slightly inebriated and had the garrulousness of a man who has just enjoyed his dinner. He spoke loudly, mumbling and repeating himself as if the words were clogging up his voice and his head.

'Old girl,' he said to the aunt as he sprawled in an armchair, 'you really should have had nephews . . . instead of nieces! Young girls, you know . . . young girls, it's not always fun in a house, when you're a bachelor . . . Tonight, for instance . . . tonight, I would have come home . . . not alone . . . that's true . . . but the fuss there would have been . . . because of the girl! . . . You would have pulled a long face! . . . Well, I believe . . . I believe in respecting young girls . . . but it's a nuisance . . . it's a nuisance . . . What I'm saying . . . you understand . . . I don't want to send that child away . . . Of course not . . . but . . . you said once that she liked that awful groom from the first floor . . . Well, that's it! Let them get married . . . because . . . a married woman . . . she can see anything, hear anything . . . whilst your blasted niece . . .'

There was the thud of a falling body against the door. Hearing the bell, Philomène, who was still on the back stairs, had recognised Monsieur Henry's ring and had come down again to say goodnight; she had used her key to come back into the apartment; she had crept silently into the corridor; she had listened, she had heard – and she had fainted on the floor.

The aunt and Monsieur Henry, who sobered up instantly, splashed her face with water and smacked her hands. When she recovered consciousness, she went into hysterics in the armchair where Monsieur Henry had seated her, in front of the open window. She ended up sobbing, to her surprise, not knowing why she was there nor why she was crying. Memory returned only after Monsieur Henry had repeated several times that he had spoken without thinking, that he wanted her to stay, that she would never go away, she could do whatever she liked, and all the soothing words one speaks to the sick.

Life in the apartment went on as if nothing had happened. Philomène seemed to have forgotten everything, and did not even show any awkwardness. After three weeks, one morning as Monsieur Henry was leaving the table, Philomène, addressing him for the first time without his having spoken to her, said in a firm and quiet tone of voice which he had never heard her use:

'Monsieur Henry, I want to apologise. I thank you very much for all your kindness to me, and for your mother's. I shall never forget it.'

And as Monsieur Henry looked surprised, she offered him her forehead:

'Will you give me a kiss, please, Monsieur Henry? To say good-bye.'

And without giving him time to interrupt, she went on at once, hurrying as if she was grasping her courage in both hands:

'Yes, I am going away. I shall leave on Monday. To become a novice in the convent of Saint Augustine. But I shall always pray for you, Monsieur Henry, for your happiness.'

Philomène was a postulant for two months in the convent of the order of Saint Augustine, clad in a black dress, with a little black bonnet. After being tested for two months with religious practices and manual labour, her religious vocation grew stronger and she was considered worthy of the novitiate. The *Veni Creator* was solemnly sung for her by the community and she came to the divine services with the white muslin veil on her head, and round her waist the wide blue sash which novices wear in the chapel and take off as they go out.

Shortly after the *Veni Creator*, she was allowed to take the habit. On that day she wore a wedding dress, the white dress which had floated for so long like a cloud in her girlhood dreams. She dressed up in all her finery in a last innocent show before her sacrifice. In the crowded chapel, she took part in high mass. The Mother Superior sat on her right, the mistress of the novices on her left, holding a lit candle symbolising the divine light which filled her soul.

After mass, 'What do you ask?' said the officiating priest.

'I beg to be admitted into this sacred house to serve God according to the rule prescribed by our holy founder, Saint Augustine.'

'Do you know it well?'

'Yes.' And Philomène recited the rule.

'Do you promise to follow it and obey it?'

'Yes, I promise to obey it, with the grace of God.'

There followed a long discourse from the officiant about the sacrifices required for the practice of a religious life, the advantages of that life, the dangers of a worldly life, the disappointments of those who search for happiness in it. Then the priest, having asked Philomène once more if she persevered in her resolution, snipped a lock of hair from her forehead. She left the chapel. When she came back, her hair was cut. The habits of the order, blessed one by one, covered her body. A cloth veil replaced the muslin veil. Her oval face was framed by the white linen which came down over her forehead and half covered it. The long, full woollen dress clothed her in thick, stiff, straight folds.

She had been given her religious name. She had been covered by a pall while the *De Profundis* was sung over her and a prayer arose from her heart – the prayer from under the pall which is said in convents to be always answered – calling for God's grace and mercy to fall over all those who had nurtured and cared for her childhood.

Three months later, the novice, who still had seven months of her novitiate to complete before taking her vows, was sent to — Hospital. She was replacing a sister who had died in a typhoid epidemic: that sister, whose death showed Philomène the way to charity, was her old friend Céline, who had become Sister Laurence.

III

The housemen were gathered in the hospital duty-room.

The stones of its vaulted ceiling were exposed by the damp. Opposite the grey-painted door, a window opened onto a courtyard two feet higher than the floor. Against the wall, to the right of the door, was a large cupboard which was used as a wardrobe and linen closet. On the left, above a brass washbowl hanging from the wall and surmounted by a towel, a large wooden rack painted black revealed in its pigeon-holes a jumble of paper bundles, notebooks and old newspapers. Then came a white earthenware stove and an untidy curtainless iron bed: the bed of the houseman on night duty. On the other side, on the bare white wall, was a large pipe-rack and the big slate on which the housemen wrote, for the attendants who came to fetch them, the ward in which they could be found. Hanging from a nail fluttered a piece of paper, showing a child's caricature of the director of the hospital. Another sheet of paper, tacked to the plaster, carried a long list of names, with ages in the margin: an alphabetical list of patients which a heart specialist had put up so he could be warned when one of them died and could attend the post-mortem.

There were seven in that room, all wearing little black skull-caps, sitting around a table on which an old woman had just placed a steaming leg of mutton. Only one of them, the houseman on duty, had kept his apron on; the other aprons hung on coat-hangers. In their buttonholes, little pink or purple pin-cushions looked like posies from a distance. They were talking.

'Poor old Lemesle, don't you know what's happened to him? He has his practice in the rue Sainte-Marguerite-Saint-Antoine. His consulting room is the wine-merchant; after each visit, they make a chalk mark on the wall. Each mark is worth a glass of wine and the merchant rubs them out as he drinks.'

'Poor chap!'

'And he was so clever!'

'I say, Dubertrand, are you going to Bicêtre for the Mid-Lent ball, to see the mad men and women dancing?'

'At what time?'

'During the day.'

'Don't go, it's no fun. It's just like a lawyer's ball. No real character.'

'But there must be some nymphomaniacs. That could be entertaining.'

'Entertaining? Believe it or not, we were surrounded once, in that sort of ball, the director, myself and Chappe, who was a non-resident student then. We couldn't get rid of them.'

'Haven't you seen them perform plays, Noël?'

'No.'

'Sometimes, when there's an epileptic enjoying himself too much, the attendants pick him up and throw him out. Weren't you with me, Pichenat?'

'Yes . . . Yes.'

'What's the matter with you this morning, Pichenat?'

'The matter? I had a scene this morning, during the consultation. I'm furious. You know my chief is in poor shape at the moment, so we have a temporary one. You can't imagine what he's like! It's lucky he won't be with us more than a fortnight. If he bothers me again tomorrow, I'll go on leave. He's a real pain! One day he comes in : "Gentlemen, get them to evacuate," and at each bed: *Ipecac, ipecac, ipecac!* The next day: "Gentlemen, we're going to use the expectorant method. Do not get them to evacuate . . ." The day after: "Gentlemen, the expectorant method is all very well for people who are well off; but do we have the right to use it in this case? Here is a cabinet-maker who needs to earn his living, to get back to work as soon as possible. Let's get them to evacuate again." And here we go: *Ipecac! ipecac!* And it goes on . . . What a Philistine!'

'Have you started your lectures, Noël?'

'Yes.'

'How many students have you got?'

'Twenty.'

'Do you have a chap called Girardeau among them?'

'Yes . . . he's all right. I think he'll get somewhere.'

'We're from the same parts. Look after him. He's been unlucky. They lost everything in '48 . . . and on top of it, his father is blind. He supports him.'

'When he walks?'

'No, by giving piano and spelling lessons in between his medical studies.'

'Monsieur Pichenat, you're wanted in Saint-Martha ward,' said the old woman who waited on them.

'Do you have any *Gazettes médicales* at home?'

'Yes, I think I've got some.'

'Will you bring them, please?'

'Who's Number 47?' asked Pichenat, coming back in.

'No idea! What do you expect. I remember the patients by bed, but not by number.'

'Barnier, have you read Runeau's thesis on Roman baths?'

'No, he hasn't sent it to me. Is it long?'

'It's a thick volume. I haven't cut the pages yet.'

'It could be interesting. But he should have taken a wider subject, made a philosophical and historical study of medicine.

Why didn't he cover the evil practices of the whole of antiquity, the scandals of the Greek and Roman world? That's the sort of framework. All the society people would read him.'

'What's happened to Thierry?'

'I've seen him today in the practical school. He wrote his thesis in three hours.'

'The devil he did!'

'He's a joker, Thierry. One day he borrowed a magnificent tumour from me under the pretext of studying it under the microscope. As he is better at it than I am, and I was short of time, I gave him everything I had. And when I asked for the analysis, he told me he intended to use it, he hadn't finished yet. A lot of nonsense!'

'Theft of a tumour! There's no law to cover it!'

There was a knock at the door.

'Come in!'

A young man came in, with long hair and a red woollen muffler. He was a candidate for the fifth-year medical exam and wanted to know the diseases of the patients about whom he would be interrogated. He was told:

'Go upstairs. There must be a houseman.'

The door closed.

'What a cheek! To ask us to deceive the examiners without even bringing a letter of recommendation from somebody!'

'He's a foxy one!'

'Madame Bizet!'

The old woman rushed forward.

'This meat here . . . Have you ever eaten human flesh?'

'Oh! Sir!'

'Well, Madame Bizet, this meat's just like it. Can you imagine precisely, Madame Bizet, the taste of human flesh?'

'How horrible! Well, I don't know . . . it must be like rabbit . . . I think.'

'No, Madame Bizet, it's a taste between beef and mutton. I'm not relying on travellers' tales, Madame Bizet. One day they brought here a woman who had tried to asphyxiate herself; she had fallen on a gas cooker. Her arm was roasted, really well done! If you cooked your chops as well as that, Madame Bizet . . .'

'Talking of chops, did you know that the management refused one to my chief, the other day, for a patient?'

'That's disgusting!'

'And what did he say, your chief?'

'He didn't say anything.'

'But he's ruthless, usually, about that sort of thing.'

'He gave ten francs to the sister to buy chops for the patient.'

'Ah! Here's the doctor!'

That was the general cry as a student who had recently taken his doctor's degree came in, carrying under his arm a bundle of his theses covered in blue paper.

'Will you have lunch?'

'Yes.'

'Madame Bizet! Bring a napkin.'

'Yes, sir,' and the old woman handed the doctor the guest napkin: a white pillow-case.

'Congratulations, old man!'

And the doctor sat down, amid handshakes, saying in a melancholy tone:

'It's no joke, you know!'

'Why?'

'To leave Paris . . .'

'Where are you going?'

'To Péronne, to open a practice. Ah! the provinces . . .'

And he started eating lugubriously.

'Ah! I understand: do you remember our first year at Bicêtre, eh, doctor? Those were the days. We had some fun. We had our rooms above old veterans of thirty years' hospital service. They didn't get much rest! We spent the nights rolling logs in the corridors. Lory played the violin as loud as he could. And then, they weren't particular about our visitors. We made punch on the roof, can you imagine . . . it sent flying stars in the Observatory telescope. And the day of the Bicêtre celebrations, we distinguished ourselves! The boys from Bicêtre wouldn't let us dance. There were more than twenty of us. The officers sided with us. We made a bit of a racket. I'm told things are different now; you're supervised, the porter reports you, they expect ladylike virtue, and no snoring at night!'

'You remember, Barnier, that blasted patient who promised to knock me down when he got out?'

'Yes, because you'd put him on a low diet . . .'

'I met him on the Pont des Arts, the other day.'

'Well?'

'Well, old man, I've cured him too well: he looked as strong as a horse to me. I crossed over to the other side of the bridge.'

A little high-pitched bell was heard, and almost at the same time the shadow of a hearse at the window took away half the daylight of the duty-room.

'Yes,' one houseman said to the doctor, 'it's still at this time, as in your old days, and in the same place . . . transfer station for eternity!'

'Hand me the brandy.'

'Which pipe do you want? The *death head* or the *lead cholics*?'

'No, the other one.'

There was a knock at the door.

'Come in!'

'Monsieur Pichenat,' said a ward maid, 'it's a woman . . . Number 14 . . . a delivery.'

'There! that always happens if you light a pipe!'

'Don't you complain! When you're in the service where I worked two years ago . . . That's a hospital where you're disturbed on duty days . . . and at night too! I worked it out: on average you're woken up seven times a night. There's that blasted step of the male nurse you hear walking in the yard, up the stairs . . . And in the morning, at six o'clock: "Knock! Knock!" "Come in!" It's a death certificate to sign. When you think that an idiot houseman gave the management the idea of requesting a check on deaths! I ask you! Patients who've been dying for two months in a ward. They've been dead a long time when you notice it; only, they insist on breathing still . . .'

'Are you pleased with operations at the moment?' the doctor asked.

'So so.'

'No, it hasn't been working well, recently.'

'That's bad luck . . .'

'The sad thing is that it doesn't depend on the surgeon. The operation might be done perfectly; but it's luck . . . like a hand at cards. You pass or you don't. It's really a question of luck.'

'Yes, it's luck. For instance, last year, my chief fell ill. He'd just done twenty-five operations in a row without any problem. Serious operations. They sent Harder to replace him. You know that Harder is as good as he is; he operates five times, the five patients die. Well, at the sixth, he pocketed his instruments and goodbye! He didn't come back.'

'He was quite right! What do you expect?'

'We're not so unlucky here as in my previous hospital. They've been losing all their operated patients for two years now. It's a nuisance, in the end. At one time, in the men's wards they had purulent infection on the third floor, tetanus on the second, and hospital gangrene on the first.'

'That's quite something!'

'The strange thing is that we lose more patients in Paris than in the provinces, where often they're butchered.'

'Come on! There are some very good surgeons in the provinces. You mustn't generalise.'

Pichenat, who had come back, was sitting in the duty chair and amusing himself by teasing his neighbour with one of the sticks stripped of their bark which the students used for mock fencing. Suddenly, the neighbour jumped from his chair onto the tablecloth.

'What are you doing, Malivoire? Climbing on the table?'

'No, I'm ascending the tribune,' the houseman called Malivoire said gravely, 'to discuss the budget. Gentlemen, there was a time, I should say a golden age, when the management enjoyed feeding us. And such was, according to the legends that have survived to our day, the management's generosity in those days, that a houseman could treat his friends with what the management gave him. Now, forced to feed ourselves, we have had to choose a cashier who seemed worthy of our esteem . . .'

'I request leave to speak!' cried Pichenat.

'It is to the behaviour of that accountant on whom we bestowed our full confidence, and who's making a bit on the side . . .'

'Quite right!'

' . . . that I want to call your attention! Pichenat – now I've named him, gentlemen – takes cabs all the time. He lets me share them, it's true, but he pays. I've seen him today talking to his boot-maker: he was paying a bill.'

'On the contrary!' said Pichenat.

'He is talking, gentlemen, about hiring a box at the Italian theatre. One word in conclusion, gentlemen . . . At Bicêtre, we lived on twenty-five francs a month. Pichenat dares ask us for eighty.'

'Why did you appoint me treasurer?'

'We appointed you so you would save money for us!'

'Malivoire! You're treading on my coffee!'

'Malivoire! Down!'

'Do we have any ink here? And a pen of sorts?' the doctor asked, and he started inscribing the copies of his thesis.

'Ah, I say! who wants a well-prepared heart? Does somebody need one?'

'It suits me. I'll have it.'

'You have a new novice in Saint-Theresa ward?'

'You haven't seen her yet?'

'No, I don't care. In my hospital last year, we had the Sisters of Saint Martha.'

'Ah yes, Jansenist sisters . . .'

'Don't mention Jansenist sisters to me. They're all pock-marked.'

'And the youngest knew our professors when they were students.'

'What's she called, our novice? They have such names . . . I don't know where they get them from.'

'Isn't she called Sister Ambroisine?'

'No, she's called Sister Philomène.'

'She's very pleasant.'

'And she seems a good sort. She doesn't scowl at you as some do.'

'A pity her nose is a bit too large.'

'Yes, but she has blue eyes and a sweet look.'

'Do you spell Métivier with an *r* or a *z* at the end?' asked the doctor, who was still writing.

'A *z*.'

'One thing about her: she's graceful. She doesn't move stupidly.'

'Well, I don't know about that . . . but she seemed charming to me. What do you say, Barnier?'

'Oh, yes, of course, she's in Saint-Theresa ward; it's Barnier's department. Well, Barnier?'

'What can I say, old man? I don't like young sisters, that's a principle with me. I hate romance. It bothers me to see little girls who imagine things and become nuns without knowing why or what for, out of romantic ideas, as they would fall in love with a cousin during the holidays. The old ones, whose hearts and hands are steady, they're all right.'

'But, old man, they must start some time.'

'That's true . . . but although I keep reminding myself of it, I can't help it. Last night, for instance, she wanted to help me with a dressing. I was afraid she'd faint, as she did once before, and I couldn't help snapping at her.'

IV

———
◆

Sister Philomène had entered the hospital with a very troubled mind. She had lived for a long time with the thought of the hospital, hoping to accustom herself to it; but that thought had become an obsession which filled her with terror. Day after day, she felt less able to resist those ideas, those dramatic images which flash into the mind of anybody walking past a high hospital wall dotted with small windows. Her imagination, feeding on the unknown, magnified the horror which must be in there. She sensed something similar to the coloured anatomy plates which she had seen as a child, somewhere in the Latin Quarter. And out of those vague ideas she built up, in spite of herself, a horrifying image.

She felt an icy touch on her temples and on her cheeks when she first entered the ward where she would train as a hospital sister. She saw, on the stoves, the pokers for stirring the fire: she mistook them for cauterising-irons. She expected to see steel instruments with ghastly stains, pieces of living flesh, all one imagines with dread about surgery!

She saw none of those things; only white beds, white curtains, white linen. Everywhere the pleasing neatness of a young girl's bedroom. Under the floor-polisher's bare feet, the flagstones shone. The patients lay back quietly on their pillows. A pretty, pinkish autumn day set off the morning whiteness of the beds against a limpid background. Lights played on the red copper of the bright, clean dishes or rested on the pale pewter of the water-jugs. Laughing housemen added a youthful note to the ward. Convalescents whispered softly. In the whole ward there was so much light, so much peace and order, a veil was so cleverly cast over the miseries and filth of all those bodies, the horror was so well concealed, suffering was so quiet and death pangs so silent that the sister was surprisingly reassured and soothed by reality. She had a feeling of liberation, confidence, joy; she thought herself rescued from the terrors of her imagination, and she was almost proud to find herself stronger than she had hoped.

Her main fear was of seeing a dead patient. She saw one who had just died. Both his hands were resting flat on the bed. A badly buttoned-up brown jersey covered his chest. Two pillows propped up his body. His head, slightly turned to one side, was thrown back. One looked down on his neck, his strong black beard, his pinched nose, his hollow eyes. Around his head, his hair stuck to his ears as if drenched in sweat. His gaping mouth had remained open in a final breath: life seemed to have stretched it in escaping. He was there, still warm, and already stiffly wrapped up in the invisible cloak of death. The sister looked at him: she remained gazing for a long time, to test herself; she felt no more emotion in front of that corpse than in front of a wax image.

She maintained herself for a few days in that state of natural firmness and effortless courage. It was a great surprise and a great satisfaction for her to be spared so easily the weakness of her senses, the flinching she had dreaded. She was beginning to feel herself hardened when, one night, looking at a patient who was asleep, quite pale, her heart failed her: she had to hold onto the bedpost so as not to fall down. Until then, through will-power, through concentrating all her strength on her work, she had avoided feeling the effect of what she saw. Now all the emotions unconsciously gathered inside her burst out without cause. She gave way to an undefined pain, to all the shocks she had not noticed before. Her nerves, kept in a state of permanent irritation by the hospital sights, now reacted with a feverish, morbid sensitivity: ordinary noises, like the dropping of a pewter tumbler, would give her a painful jolt.

Every day now she saw a little more of what the hospital hides so admirably from a first glance. The heads of the young students leaning, at consultation time, over a bed, were sometimes not close enough to prevent her catching sight between them, in spite of herself, of a raw, bleeding sore. Every hour she came across death in that horrible brown box, carried by two male nurses, hiding the corpse and adding the awe of mystery to the terror of death. A variety of objects, meaningless to her at first, now acquired a significance which took hold of her mind as she went by. She could not see them without recalling a frightening memory, a painful sight. Objects called up the shadows of the sufferings they had touched. On the upturned wooden stretcher, in the hall outside the ward, she could see the pale-looking women who, nearly every day, were carried to the operating theatre, and brought back even paler. She then felt a constraint under her ribs, her legs grew weak and her bones seemed to freeze from the knees to the tops of her toes.

At the top of the curving staircase up and down which she went so often to go in and out of Saint-Theresa ward, there was a wide landing, and on that landing, a wall near which she had to walk. When her skirt touched it, she was filled with terror, like a child at night. It was a wall like all other walls, without even the brown marks left by a bleeding hand which could be seen on some other walls in the hospital: but she knew that behind it was the operating theatre.

V

◆

The hospital, its wards, its beds, soon became for her like that wall: what her eyes did not see, her thoughts conjured up. Her imagination took her behind the curtains, under the sheets, like a hateful second sight which intervening veils exacerbated without impeding. Sometimes, tormented by that unceasing awareness, she felt tears rising to her eyes. She held them back, but they rose again a moment later. Banal scenes, the most ordinary incidents of hospital life, noises, sights devoid of any drama, unexpectedly made her feel faint. The smallest thing was enough to bring those tears to her eyes, that faintness to her heart: in her sensitive state, her courage failed her.

Emotions affected her body like a great weariness, which exhausted her as a night's play exhausts a gambler. Her tired senses let her down, and her will was crushed so that she could have cried out: *Enough! Enough for today!* Then she would force herself to move, walk, act. She would rush around under some pretext; she would perform an unnecessary duty; thus her reconquered strength began to obey her again.

At night, when she was not on duty at the hospital, she went back to the convent with an empty head, heavy, dull thoughts, unable to concentrate or move. She had difficulty in following the meaning of prayers, in finding words for them. Her brain only worked mechanically, following her physical sensations. Images came to her, to which she surrendered in lazy, absorbed contemplation; strange illusory images which brought pitilessly to her mind the living reality. She refused to see them, she prayed . . . But the smell came back, the unbearable smell absorbed by her clothes, soaked up by her skin: she not only saw the hospital, she was there!

For a long time, she struggled and suffered thus, trying to conquer herself, offering her suffering to God and asking Him every day for the steadfastness of routine.

VI

◆

In hospitals there is a time around ten o'clock in the morning which is, because of its noises, its comings and goings, the ebullience of the patients, the life of the wards, quite unlike other times: almost cheerful. It is a sort of truce. The doctors' rounds, the dressings, are over. The physician's presence and words have brought hope closer to each bed; the gentle, skilful hand of the houseman has given the relief of a new dressing, a fresh liniment. Bodies and souls have been comforted. The ward orderly, leaning forward, is dragging away soiled linen in a large sheet which she pulls behind her with both hands. Between the beds a brush is tracing patches of light on the floor. On the fat white pillows, heads are resting; faces are calm and smiling, half alive again, with a confident, cheerful look. On chairs at the heads of the beds, the fitter patients are dressing, sitting sideways, half turned towards the window, happy and weary as though getting up for the first time, slowly, stopping now and then and vaguely gazing in front of them. Soon, out of the dispensary comes a large basket full of golden loaves on each of which a knife has marked four shares; and also a little trolley bearing, on a white napkin, the ward lunch.

First, Sister Philomène carried the broth from one patient to the next. Light and quick, she went from bed to bed, holding in front of her the pewter bowl whose steam rose to her face. In a second she was at the head of the bed, on the right of the reclining patient. To some, she left the broth; weaker ones, who painfully hoisted themselves up as they saw her, she helped to drink, holding up with one hand their bent heads, and with the other, outstretched, lifting up to their lips the warm bowl which trembled in their nerveless hands. After the broth she handed out the bread, more swiftly still, with a lighter, flying haste which made her veil float behind her and her dress brush against the curtains. She was at one bed, then immediately at another, flitting by. Wearing a grey cowl, a convalescent patient followed her; arching her waist in her square woollen dress, she carried the loaves in a large tablecloth suspended round her neck by a large knot and held in front of her with one straining arm outlined within the folds of material. By each bed the convalescent opened up the tablecloth for the sister, who grasped one piece of bread for each patient and swiftly put it down at the foot of the bed, on the cover. Then came the wine, which another convalescent held out to her in a wooden pail; and the sister, by each bed, dipped into the pail the smallest of the tin measures. Once, twice, three times, she filled and poured the measure into the drinking mug, glancing at the same time at the sheet of paper fastened to her sleeve which indicated the wine ration for each bed. And the clinking of metal on the bedside tables followed her step, ran behind her to the end of the ward.

After the wine, the sister handed out to the patients who were not yet on a full convalescent diet the more delicate food allotted to them: chicken, cutlets, jam. The ward orderly or some woman able to get up helped her in that duty; then she dragged and pushed the little trolley, stopping now and then with the large rice-pudding basin, the dish of stewed prunes and a few portions of boiled beef which looked minute on the large tin tray.

During all that time, Sister Philomène busied herself happily. So lively that she seemed to have wings, so beautiful in her kindness, with her sleeves tucked up for work over her white hands, she went hither and thither, gently teasing the patients about their appetite, laughing at their hunger, promising one to recommend her for an extra portion, another, if she was good, to bring her some tit-bit the next day, thinking of everything, sweeping away with her fingers the crumbs which had dropped on the sheets.

For Sister Philomène, this was the best part of her day. She forgot herself, she found new strength in that welcome tiredness. She was able to put out of her mind all the ugly, frightening things around her. The morning filled her soul and often gave her courage for the rest of the day.

VII

To the strength she drew from that hour and from the morning activities was added another, livelier strength, whose source within herself renewed itself inexhaustibly, as though from divine grace. That strength was nothing more than the blessing of her heart, an illusion which sustains, at the beginning, medical students as well as sisters against repugnance. The sister believed she was doing much to fight death, to improve the health of her patients. She had the credulous, generous faith, the beautiful intoxicating charity which God gives to those who first come into contact with illness, so they can proceed without weakening until they have become accustomed to it. Sister Philomène believed that suffering could not withstand her care, her vigilance, her attentiveness, the effort of all her thoughts, the will-power of her whole being. She hoped to create miracles by giving her life to the sick, by watching even over their sleep, by reporting their state to the physician, by calling at the slightest accident for the attention and experience of the houseman, by checking their medicines and dispensing them herself, by making their cure her one thought and the business of every minute. She believed she could tear them away from disease by enveloping them in tenderness: she would talk to them, she would smile, she would conquer their despair, she would lift them towards hope; she would be a sister by the bedside, she would be a mother's prayer for solitary dying patients with neither family nor home: death would not take life from her arms.

That was a dream of which time and reality soon revealed the futility. The sister realised that life and death are not in human hands. She saw that the last hour is irrevocable, and that neither prayer nor care can disarm nature. And if her duty did not lessen in her eyes, her mission appeared more modest, limited to the lightening of human suffering. But when that disappointment came to her, when that truth was revealed at the end of long months of struggle and worry, she had already been toughened; she no longer needed the prop or deceit of an illusion in order to follow her chosen path without weakening. Her nervous sensitivity had worn out with her early zeal. Sickness and death had become customary, and no longer made her glance waver, her hand weaken, her heart recoil. All that was left of the woman in her was conquered and mastered by the sister and, strong in her habit as within armour, she knelt down in front of the glazed recess where she sat during the day, at the end of the ward, and thanked God with a joyful heart.

From that time she was strong and serene, but not hardened. Her even and constant gentleness did not become routine: she remained tender. The patients requested her care because she came to them with a look of compassion and interest. They loved her because of her glance, which spoke to them, because of her voice, which touched them so delicately. They loved her because some emotion still fluttered within her dedication.

VIII

<hr>

'Ah! Did you really find it so hard to get used to the hospital? You, a doctor, a man!'

'Yes. People think it's easy for us. Now, myself, for instance, and I'm not the only one, for nearly fifteen months, when I started my resident training, I was sad – deeply sad – and there always remains something. If I told you that it was six months before I could eat with an appetite!'

'Ah! I'm so glad you told me that. One is so ashamed of oneself at the beginning.'

'And for us it's even more horrible than for you. The first time you cut into the flesh of a dead man in the theatre . . . I assure you it has an effect on you. It gives you quite a turn. And post-mortems! When you have to search in all that stuff! And the smell which sticks to your hands and which you carry with you everywhere. Luckily there's mustard seed to wash with. Yes, it's tough at first, you know, for everybody. This morning in fact, we had a scene. As we'd carried on a little the other day at the school, we thought we recognised an informer at the consultation. A very correct informer, very neat, young, with a little dark moustache. We pushed him gradually against a bed where there was a smallpox patient . . . and bang! He fell down flat, so we said: "There's one!" '

Barnier, the houseman of Saint-Theresa ward, was chatting with Sister Philomène. The sister listened to him, looking at him in the shadow of the open door as he leant one shoulder against the door jamb. Standing in the middle of her little office, she was all lit up in front of him. Daylight flooded in through the panes of the large window, surrounding her and making her white dress dazzle. From all sides of the recess, through the glass and the curtains, the sun was reflected and glimmered over her. In that brightness which enfolded her, her face was framed by the transparent head-dress and veil, as by a halo. Her complexion had the whiteness of transfiguration which the cloister sometimes lends to nuns, that virginal and divine radiance which is reminiscent of the glory of a resurrected body. Her face glowed with heavenly health.

'You give me courage,' she said after a moment's silence. 'Ah! you're looking at the book I have been reading. I wanted to ask you . . . You will have to explain many things to me.'

'Ah! very good . . . it's the *Handbook*. But of course, Mother, I am at your service.'

'You see, one needs to know . . . One has to learn a little medicine if one wants to be of some use to the patients. Oh! I don't want to be sent away again like the other day, you know – when you took that dressing out of my hands.'

'Was I such a brute?'

'Why do you ask?'

'Because you're still angry with me.'

'No . . . or I wouldn't mention it. You didn't trust me, I know. But now I'm strong. I have prayed so much that strength has been given to me. Put me to the test, you'll see.'

IX

The great victory, the new control the sister had over herself were not absolute at first. She still had to fight to keep them. From time to time she was still unexpectedly overcome by the feelings and impressions from which she thought she had freed herself. And then she found fresh reasons to be upset.

One morning, as she was walking down to the linen room, she saw the houseman going into the consulting room. Remembering that she wanted to ask him about the dose of quinine to be given to a patient, she decided to go and talk to him where he was. She walked across the snow-covered courtyard, following the light trace of footsteps which formed, along the thawing gutter, a narrow path to the stairs into the ward, and she entered the surgery office.

By the light of the uncurtained window, over the wooden gate beyond which patients were queuing up, an old man was showing the physician a swelling like a large knot on his thin wrist. He was a poor little old man all shrivelled by the cold in a shiny, worn-out overcoat with the collar turned up. Long, straggly white hair hung over his bony face; his hollow eyes were a mere glimmer. He stood, stooping, humble, with his hat shaking in his hand. He was shaking too, like a dead tree battered by the winter wind. Barnier looked at the patient's wrist:

'You have a cough?' he asked, without looking up.

'Yes, sir, all the time,' the old man answered, with a voice like an exhausted breath. 'But my wrist is aching.'

'But . . . but we can't treat you here. You must go to the square in front of Notre-Dame.' The old man was silent, looking at the houseman. 'And ask for medicine, not surgery, medicine.' the houseman repeated, since his patient did not seem to hear.

'But that's where it hurts,' the old man said in his weak voice, showing his wrist.

'They'll look after that too, when they cure your cough.'

'On the square in front of Notre-Dame!' shouted in the old man's ear a loud voice which came out of a thick moustache and raised itself to avoid becoming moved: it was the hospital porter, standing stock still behind the old man, with his hands behind his back.

Out of the window, one could see the snow falling in thick flakes. The old man went away silently, hat in hand, still shaking.

'Poor devil! What weather! It's a long way,' said the porter, looking at the snow. 'He may only have about five days to live.'

The houseman had turned round to a young man who was standing next to him.

'Yes, it's hard, sometimes. But if I'd taken him in, my chief would have sent him away again tomorrow. It's not easy to find a place for those poor chaps. He's what we call in hospital slang an *old crock*. If we took in all the consumptives . . . Paris is a city which wears people out! We'd have no room left for the others, the ones we *can* cure.' Then, seeing that the sister was waiting to speak to him: 'What can I do for you, Mother?'

'I don't know, I've forgotten,' the sister mumbled, and she ran away.

X

'Madame One!'

'Madame Six!'

'Madame Eleven! Listen! I want to tell you something . . .'

The patients in Saint-Theresa ward were calling each other by their bed numbers, answering and chattering. They were almost all in their beds. Seven or eight, just getting up, sat on the chairs by the beds. Some were shuffling along with short steps. One, sitting at the end of the large table, was writing under the dictation of another woman, with the straining of the elbows and stiffening of the body of uneducated people who are not used to writing and make hard work of it. The houseman was finishing his four o'clock consultation.

From one bed to the next, you could hear:

'Will you have visitors tomorrow?'

'Tomorrow? Ah yes! It's Thursday. I don't know.'

'I'm expecting three people . . . no, four,' said a woman, counting on her fingers. 'You didn't see my husband last time, did you?'

'Yes, I saw him. Do you think I was asleep, with a thing like that on my stomach?'

'And you?'

'Oh, not me! My husband and my children would have to travel seventy leagues.'

'You come from so far away?'

'That's right. Not from your Paris, thank goodness! I wouldn't stay here if I could help it. Not a single tree in front of the churches! If you have relatives here, that's all right, but others only come here for the hospital. And that's no fun! It's so ugly here! I'm sure I'll still feel sad for a fortnight when I get home.'

'Is it so nice, then, where you live?'

'Is it nice? Look: the main street is here, you see. Well, we're just there. You go in . . . That's the best room . . . Oh! I'll have some work to clean up! Men, you know . . . Then there are two bedrooms behind, and the garden. And on your left, in the garden, the shed. That's where Dad and the children work at their knives. They make cutlery, good stuff, which they sell in the rue de Richelieu. They work like horses! So, there's the garden . . . We have a pear tree which is loaded every year. We have to throw away some of the fruit! Then, at the end, the river, with such clear water! You only have a few steps to go to do your washing.'

'I say, Madame Nine, were you here when there was that ragman's wife?'

'No.'

'Imagine, that poor woman had started her last throes on the Sunday morning. Her husband comes to visit her during the day — a horrible man who spent his time drinking. He'd already drunk all she had. She'd saved a few francs and knotted them in her shift. That bastard, pretending to embrace her, tries to get hold of them. She cries out: "Stop thief!" There was quite an uproar in the ward.'

The houseman had reached the last beds. Passing one of them, he gently scratched the blanket, near the foot.

'I'm not ticklish any more, Monsieur Barnier,' said, almost cheerfully, the woman who had just had a leg amputated. After a moment's silence, she went on talking to a neighbour:

'That's a fact, there are bad men, but there are good ones too. Monsieur Barnier here is gentle, and he cares about the patients.

It's half past, isn't it? So! isn't our sister going to do her orange walk today? It would really freshen my mouth, a slice of orange.'

'The sister? Yes, here she is. She's coming out of her box.'

Sister Philomène had just come out of her office. As she walked, she held out at arm's length, away from her dress, an orange which she was peeling. Having removed the rind, she slowly skinned the slices, then, coming up to the bedheads, she popped into the mouths of the reclining women, open and expectant like children's mouths, one slice each, translucent between her white fingers.

At the name of Barnier, praise of the houseman ran across the ward. Gratitude was general, blessings were uttered.

'Yes, a decent young man. And he doesn't grudge his work.'

'He really knows how to do a dressing! With warm water first, so it doesn't hurt at all.'

'He visited my husband at home . . . not that it pays him much.'

All those echoing voices softly reached Sister Philomène. She had slowed down her step; and she felt an involuntary liking for the women who were speaking in that way.

'Here are some paper cornets. I hope the dispensary will be satisfied.' The speaker was addressing a patient, lying in bed with a large cat sleeping peacefully on her feet. 'Tomorrow! Tomorrow!' and she repeated the word once more, as a sing-song. 'I shall try to get my certificate from the ward orderly today, so I can leave in the morning. To see my little home . . . I'm so happy! When your turn comes, my girl, you'll see; your legs may be weak, but you feel strong enough to go away! Never mind: we should all go on the same day. It's a pity to leave one's friends behind.'

'Oh! *I* don't mind staying: I'm not in pain any more. You see, that's the main thing, not to suffer, when you've been in pain as I have. And then, I asked one of my visitors to read my fortune in coffee dregs. She saw me standing on both legs in a few months . . . and that's a woman who had told me all that was going to happen to me. I've still got something, I can work: it takes the boredom away.'

'It looks really nice, your embroidery. Worthy of a princess, isn't it?'

'I'll tell you,' the patient said after looking to see if Sister Philomène was nearby, 'it's for a present. It's a petticoat inset. I've been here six months now. Monsier Barnier has looked after me so well, I thought of giving him a little souvenir. That young man is too nice not to have a girlfriend. So, that will make a petticoat for her. It's pretty, when you go dancing.'

'Have you finished chattering? Do you want to get a fever?' said Sister Philomène, looking almost stern.

XI

So many things, so many duties are left to the judgement, the good will and the zeal of the sisters by the hospital administration that a sister in a hospital ward can be everything or nothing. She is nothing if she lacks initiative and keenness, if she lacks the energy and youthfulness of dedication. Even if she is pious and virtuous, she is nothing if she lacks the natural gift of using her hands and her soul to help the patients. She is nothing without a delicacy which allows her to soften the hearts of those who suffer, without a sort of motherly authority through which she understands the needs, the thoughts, the confidence of men and women of the people. Or if she has been deprived of the providential gifts which prepare her for that role: if she lacks physical strength and health, if her face is not one of those smiling, pleasant faces which illness likes to see by its bedside – then she is only a ward orderly gentler than other orderlies. But if she is endowed with those charms, if she is active and sympathetic, always ready to work, and if she widens, because of her large heart, the restricted scope of her duties, if she tries to make her task as great as her dedication, if she is really a charity sister, she is everything, she does everything, she is capable of everything in the ward.

To receive the medicines brought to the dispensary by the houseman, to check them, to administer them, to distribute food and wine, to keep the wine safe from the male nurses and the maids, to deliver the linen, to share with the ward orderly the care of the patients, to keep order in the ward – those are the sister's only official duties. But those general attributions, put into her hands, if she wants to use them to the full, mean the whole governing of the ward. For instance, next to the distribution of food and wine, there is the granting of tokens, the supplementary allowance of wine, of fish, of jam; small comforts granted to convalescents with a capricious appetite, which the sister can always obtain from the doctor if she knows how to ask. Her strict duties do not go beyond the administering of medicines, the sharing of patient care; but is she forbidden to do more than the work of a ward orderly? Through watching the patients closely, through experience, through the study of a little elementary medicine, can she not help the doctor with her observations, call the physician in time, nurse the patients with some knowledge of their illness? Beyond the material care of the ward, the ensuring of cleanliness and order, is she not entitled to a moral care? Is it not her duty to note which convalescents sell their bread, to listen to the patients' complaints, to take those complaints to the management? Her duty to report those among the nurses and orderlies who demand a tip for the care they give?

Of all the sister's duties, isn't the comforting of the sick the greatest? She is in charge of those suffering souls, she must bring hope to those beds where the dead are replaced in quick succession by the sick. And what greater duty could there be: to remind the patients of Providence, to make them forget the poverty of their homes, to show the future to some, heaven to others, to place piously joined hands beside those for whom nobody prays, to spare the dying the thought of the operating theatre, to soothe with thoughts of God the last breath of life!

In the ward where she had been placed under the direction of a good, devoted, but old mother, the young novice, winning over by her charm and her zeal the doctor and his students, soon rose to the responsible post of hospital sister. Fully in charge under a superior who was devoid of jealousy and glad to be relieved, she acquired experience, and her merciful influence grew day by day.

She was the intermediary through whom all that was hard in the hospital rule could be softened, the kind, light hand by which suffering longed to be touched, the lulling, serene voice which brought courage to convalescence. She was the watchfulness and control which made the service in the ward humane and conscientious. She was almost a family for the patients, because she shared in their loves as a confidante, in their thoughts as a relative, in their tears as a friend. She was always to be seen walking from one bed to the next, going from one patient to the other, from the dispensary to the ward, from the ward to her office, adding, controlling, checking, bent over registers, without stopping or taking time to sit down. Her habit went back and forth, always in motion.

She was loved and revered. The old residents of the ward told new patients of their luck, of the good sister they were going to have. Even in other wards they noted which nights she was on duty. In the evenings, they looked forward to her round; and when, during the day, she went down the stairs, the convalescents who, on the landing of the men's ward, smoked a pipe whilst trying out their crutches, saluted her by doffing their nightcaps. She was popular. Her name cropped up at students' dinners: some mentioned her gracefulness with enthusiasm, others with curiosity. And deep down, all of them, doctors and housemen, felt proud of their admirable sister, the novice of Saint-Theresa ward.

XII

When, in a pauper hospital, the patient, man or woman, is not a rough creature, a sort of animal with hardened instincts which poverty has made wild; when he shows humane characteristics and a moral sensibility under caring hands; when his heart has been refined by a beginning of education, that patient finds that doctors and housemen give him particular care.

Sisters also are attracted in spite of themselves to those who will best reward their tenderness, to souls in which they can sow God's seed.

Devotion to her grateful patients sustained Sister Philomène's courage. They were her strength and her forbearance. Sometimes she reproached herself for it; she told herself, in moments of stern self-examination, that her preferences were unfair; but as she felt no remorse, she judged that God was not asking her to sacrifice them. Were they not her whole life, these affections born by a bedside and too often ended at the same bedside by death? Was it not her only comfort, the adoption of those women whom she would see, after long anguished days, walk away one morning cheerfully recovered, turn the doorknob and disappear, leaving her both a great joy and the heartbreak of loss?

Sister Philomène had among her patients a woman, still young, whom they had expected to cure at first, but whose state had become hopeless. The language, the behaviour of that woman, who never talked of her past, betrayed what remained of the beginning of a happy life, of an education, of a fortune. One guessed at her downfall, one of those unhappy combinations of circumstances which force white hands to turn to work. Her moving thanks, her deep but restrained despair, her resignation, had attracted the interest of all – of the surgeon, of the housemen, of the other patients. Every day, availing himself of the visiting rights granted by the hospital to the sons and daughters of patients, a little boy, who was soon discovered to come from furnished apartments in the rue de l'Hôtel de Ville, came to sit at the bedside of the poor woman, whom he called Mummy. His clothes had the look of worn-out rich children's garments which he had outgrown. He would remain seated on the high chair, next to the bed, his legs dangling, holding back his tears, staring at his mother who, too weak to speak to him, would gaze at him passionately for a long hour, then send him home.

Sister Philomène had become attached to the child. Every day she had a piece of fruit, a sweet to give him, a surprise for him. She led him by the hand into her office. There, she talked to him; she showed him pictures in a religious book or amused him by giving him a pencil, sitting him at her desk and letting him scribble on blank tokens. Sometimes she washed his face, combed his hair and brought him back, clean and tidy, to the patient's bedside. The mother looked at the sister as she would have looked at the Virgin Mary if she had appeared holding the child by the hand.

The woman grew weaker and weaker. One day, the child was on the chair next to her. He was looking at her, almost frightened, searching for his mother in that face which he no longer recognised. The sister was fondling him and trying to amuse him. Barnier, at the foot of the bed, was putting poultices on the patient's legs, under the sheets. And the sick woman, turned towards the sister, was saying, with the soft, slow, penetrating voice of the dying:

'No, mother, it's not ... death ... which frightens me. I am ready ... if it were only me ... but him, mother ...' and she glanced towards the child, 'when I am no longer here . . . a child . . . and so young . . . what will become of him?'

'But,' said Sister Philomène, 'you will recover. We shall save you, won't we, Monsieur Barnier?'

'Certainly . . . we shall save you,' said the houseman in a strained voice.

'Oh!' said the patient, with a woeful smile, half closing her eyes. 'You see, mother, you can't know . . . a poor child left all alone . . . I was all he had . . .'

'My sister, you have Christian feelings which must not allow you to doubt God's goodness, His mercy. God will not abandon your child.'

And Sister Philomène, uttering an exhortation which became a prayer, seemed, above the dying woman's bed, to lift up in her arms and offer to God the misery of an orphan.

When she had spoken, the patient remained silent for a while, then sighed:

'Yes, mother, I know . . . but to go away . . . without knowing . . . if I was sure he would at least have enough to eat . . . yes, bread . . . if at least I was told he would have bread!' And tears poured out of her eyes, which death was beginning to dim.

Barnier, having applied poultices, had remained leaning against the bed, his feet rooted to the ground, his back to the dying woman's tears. His hands, behind him, were nervously toying with the iron bedpost when suddenly, carried away by one of those impulses which overwhelm the hearts of even the strongest, he turned round and said in a rough voice:

'Well, if that's all you need, you needn't worry. I have a good old mother who lives in the country. The house seems larger now that I've left. It's as easy as winking. Your kid will keep her company. And I promise you she doesn't make children unhappy.'

'Oh!' said the patient, reviving, 'The good Lord will reward you!'

And she clasped her child eagerly as if, before leaving him to another woman, she wanted him to feel right to the bottom of his soul his mother's last embrace.

'Yes,' the sister repeated, looking at the houseman, 'the good Lord will reward you.'

XIII

◆

Sister Philomène had become accustomed to the hospital. She soon began to enjoy her work. That life shut up in a sickroom acquired for her, with time, a strange charm. She grew fond of that existence, of the place where all her time was spent, where her heart could spend itself in dedication, of the narrow circle within which her days revolved. The world and its upheavals were only a whisper which died out around her and which she no longer heard. Those walls, those beds, those reclining women were the horizon of her sight and the horizon of her soul: she looked for nothing else, dreamt of nothing beyond it. And her life in the hospital ward gave her the calm, the serenity of a country vicarage garden bordered by a churchyard.

Peace, an infinite peace, was hers. Sacrifice, work, a life full of duties had regulated and strengthened her religious feelings. Her faith had been crowned and rewarded by the unceasing fervour which the lively, feverish faith of her childhood and youth had for so long sought in vain from God with the straining, the violence, the impatience of a human passion. She no longer needed to conjure up God's presence: she found it always companionably by her side. The fears, the troubles, the bitterness of her past frailness were left far behind: her soul had the same health as her body, the same serenity as her face, and she enjoyed that full possession of grace with nothing threatened, seeking ceaselessly and endlessly from divine love, as from the inexhaustible source from which

Saint Catherine used to fill her glass, the gifts and charms of earthly beatitude, the radiant joy, the smiling love which give a woman an angel's halo.

Everything was fulfilled within her. Her sensitivity, once so easily exalted and ready to turn into love, her tender instincts so cruelly wounded by indifference and scorn, had been soothed, satisfied, used by charity, with its duties and delights. When, after spending the whole day tending the limbs and the wounds of Jesus Christ in the limbs and wounds of the poor, the sister, her task over, slowly went up to her cell, she saw again in thought the relief her hands and her words had given, the sufferings she had lulled, the hope she had given, the goodness she had taken from bed to bed, the life she had prolonged, the death she had comforted; she seemed to carry to her own bedside the thankful glances, the grateful words of all her patients. And then she felt rising within her an unutterable joy, a joy which was not earthly, a joy which was unlike any of the human happinesses or pleasures, a joy which made her heart swell inside her breast and which delighted her like the triumphal song of her conscience.

XIV

The child adopted by Barnier's mother, 'the kid', as Barnier called him, had become a link between the sister and the houseman, a common interest which brought them together. Their thoughts met over his small head: 'My mother has written . . . the kid sends you a kiss,' Barnier would say, as he walked past the sister, during the morning consultation. Soon, a chat would follow that brief announcement. To childish messages, to the jokes exchanged between housemen and sisters as they met in a ward, succeeded short talks, sometimes light-hearted, sometimes serious, about the hospital and the patients. When the afternoon dressing did not take too long and Barnier had some time to himself, he would walk into the sister's office; and there, sitting on the chair next to her straw-bottomed armchair, he talked with her, sometimes for a whole quarter of an hour. The sister, concerned about her patients, would question him about technical terms in the *Handbook*, ask him how a potion, a medicine had to be administered, and nearly always they found themselves talking about what still had to be done to reach, in hospitals, a more perfect charity, a more complete realisation of the ideal. They exchanged ideas about improvements; fired by such a beautiful dream, the sister would entrust the future to the houseman, when one day he would be a great surgeon at the head of a hospital. Air would have to be renewed more often: all that was needed was a ventilation system which, without bringing in the cold, would take out stale air and introduce clean air; the sister complained that pewter did not keep herbal teas warm enough, that it should be replaced by coarse china, even if it meant a few breakages; the dead should be removed in a less obvious, less visible way for their neighbours, a less horrible way than that frightful box: on a camp-bed, for instance, like the patients due for an operation; the male nurses and ward orderlies should be paid more than twelve francs per month if one required them to be honest instead of trying to make money out of the living and the dead by charging the patients and robbing the corpses . . . There were all kinds of reforms – large and small – of customs and regulations on which, in their utopian zeal, the sister and the houseman would build their model hospital.

One afternoon they had talked of all those things longer than usual:

'Monsieur Barnier,' the sister said as she stood up, 'you must promise me something . . .'

'Tell me, Mother.'

'When you are a great surgeon . . .' Barnier smiled at those words, which the sister often used, ' . . . if I'm still alive . . . I'll be just the same, I'll wear a black veil, that's all, and I'll still be in a hospital . . . Well! one never knows . . . by chance . . . if I find myself in one of your wards . . . I want you to promise me never to refuse me any favours for my patients . . .'

'If that's all,' Barnier said, and he stretched out his hand, 'I swear I shall bankrupt the hospital management with chicken wings, Bagnols wine and fried mackerel.'

XV

Those talks, which she enjoyed and which were renewed under thousands of pretexts, soon grew longer and more confidential. They became, for the sister, a welcome recreation. It was a break in her day, something unexpected in her life, a breath of outside air. She felt invigorated by that exchange of thoughts which interrupted her duties, which allowed her an expansiveness of which the hospital had deprived her. And she enjoyed listening to the houseman, who focused on so many things his memories, his curiosity, his ignorance, his imagination. She approached those talks with an openness which removed from her any constraint, any embarrassment, any false humility. She chatted with him familiarly, almost fraternally. Often, she asked questions whose naïveté puzzled him.

She let words slip out, in her innocence. As her thoughts were pure, she expressed herself in the full ingenuousness of her conscience. Candour flowed from her.

She not only had the bold frankness of a virgin; through charity, which brought her into contact with men as well as women, through the daily practice of a dedicated service which had filled her heart with a courage unusual in a woman, she had acquired in the hospital the free speech, the manly vocabulary − strange, but not without charm − of hospital sisters.

XVI

From hospital matters, their conversation gradually moved to outside things. The sister asked Barnier for news of that world which surrounded her and which she no longer knew, of that Paris whose noise she heard at night from her cell, dying away in a distant rumbling of carriages. She wanted to know what had changed since her time, what was no longer as she knew it, the places where she had been taken for walks, her old childhood haunts, the Tuileries, the Champs-Elysées; all she found by searching among half-erased memories, like a blind girl asking about the town where she was born and which she would never see again.

What reached her from outside like a faint echo gave her cause for more questions: she asked the houseman about a new church being built, a military review, a new street in a district she had crossed, a dinner to which he had been invited by his chief, a murderer whose name she had heard mentioned by the patients, the carnival with all the mummers, the most varied and contradictory things. The houseman was very much amused by the sister's questions, which were those of a child or a prisoner: and, playing on her credulity, he would sometimes invent such tall stories that he had to stop in the middle, laughing.

'Ah! that's clever,' she would say, slightly hurt. 'To play tricks on somebody who knows nothing about what is going on.'

One day, in the course of the conversation, he told her he had crossed the rue de la Chaussée d'Antin. She asked at once if he had not seen such and such a house, towards the middle of the street, at such and such a number, if such and such a name was no longer on the shop on the left, if there was still a stationer next to the china shop.

'Really, Mother,' the houseman said with a smile, 'do you think I carry in my head all the houses of the streets where I walk?'

'But *I* see them,' the sister answered naïvely.

'Well, if you like, I'll go that way again on Wednesday and I promise you I shall look.'

'Ah! good. You will remember the number? You will see if there is still in the shop, next to the door, a big man with short arms . . . and in the other one a little girl . . . she must be a big girl now . . . She had red hair, it's not difficult . . . You will look at the fourth floor . . . I would cry if I saw the windows again,' the sister said, as if talking to herself. 'I was there as a child,' she went on, emerging from her daydream.

XVII

Sometimes the houseman felt like teasing her. He would pester Sister Philomène about religion. He argued, he philosophised, he debated with mischievous stubbornness, but lightly, like a polite man laughing at the tastes of a girl he worships or the convictions of a woman he respects. He baited the sister, he badgered her jokingly to make her answer. He would have liked to annoy her. But the sister could guess what he wanted from the smile which his eyes could not conceal. She would let him talk, look at him and start laughing. The houseman would sternly take up his arguments again, looking for those which would worry the sister most, trying for instance to prove the physical impossibility of some miracle with scientific arguments. The sister, undisturbed, answered with a joke, a common-sense remark, one of the simple words which faith provides for the ignorant and the simple. His patience exhausted, Barnier said to her one day:

'Well, Mother, if there is no heaven, you must admit you are in for quite a surprise!'

'Yes,' answered Sister Philomène, laughing, 'but if there is, *you're* the one who will be surprised!'

XVIII

◆

'I've seen your patient, Mother, she'll be up in a week. I'm full of good news today: there's no case of erysipelas among the patients who have been operated on this morning. Aren't you pleased to know that Number 25 is out of danger?'

'Oh! the poor woman! Don't I look pleased?'

'Yes . . . yes . . . but not like other days.'

'You may be right, Monsieur Barnier . . . Today I have a reason to be sad.'

She stopped, then, as the houseman remained silent:

'Oh! my goodness! It's not a secret. You know, as a sister, one mustn't get too fond of anything. That's why we are often moved from one ward to another while we are novices. Well, I knew it was to be expected . . . I often thought about it . . . But all the same, when I was told I might be moved to the men's ward, I felt strange . . . it hurt . . . I can't tell you . . . I'm used to my ward, to my patients, to the faces, to my little office, to . . . all this. Another ward will no longer be my ward, nor my patients . . . It's wrong to think that way, I know, but I can't help it.'

'It's not decided yet?'

'No, not yet . . . but I'm afraid.'

'Then we're both in suspense. But in my case it won't just be a change of ward, but of hospital. In a few months I'll reach the end of my two years as a houseman here. I'll have to go somewhere else. I'll be shifted, one of these days. Like you, it worries me a little, to change. I know that if I exerted myself, if I asked, as the management is pleased with me, I might be allowed to stay a third year as a favour.'

'Ah! You too are sorry to go?' the sister said. 'But you,' she went on after a moment's silence, with her face bent down, 'you, it's not the same. For us it's a duty to leave, when it hurts us not to stay, when we're accustomed to a place. But you have no such reasons. You must ask to stay, Monsieur Barnier . . . That would be a nice task for me, having to tell the patients that you were going away. What a reception I'd get!'

XIX

'Yes, we had fun,' the houseman was telling the sister. 'We spent the day in the woods at Meudon. We were with Malivoire, the houseman of Saint-John ward, and . . . and me. We came back through Bellevue. At the end of the Castle Avenue we turned right into a lane, a charming little lane. There was the Seine down below, we could see it through the trees. Evening was falling . . . it was beautiful. And we came back in a boat, as far as Neuilly. The night was so mild! It's very pretty, down Bellevue way.'

'Ah! It's pretty?'

'You've never been there?'

'No, I only know Saint-Cloud. Is it more beautiful?'

'More beautiful? It's more cheerful. There's a view. Do you know Saint-Germain?'

'No.'

'Ah! That's where you have a view. From the bank you can see many leagues away, as on a map. You mean you've only been to Saint-Cloud?'

'Yes.'

'There are such pretty places! Chatou, for instance . . . and all round. All you have to do is get out of Paris and walk straight on. Bougival, that's delightful too. I could go on till tomorrow, giving you names of places I remember, all green, full of trees, with water . . . places that look happy, I give you my word! And where bad wine tastes good.'

'I'll never see all that,' said the sister.

XX

The sister, in her office, resting one knee on her armchair, was briskly drawing a small feather-duster along the black frame of a coloured lithograph of Saint Theresa, over the bundles of string hanging from the frame of the glass partition, over the top of the little mahogany desk, over the water decanter covered with a glass. Barnier went past the door. Half turning her head, she called out over her shoulder:

'I'm staying.'

And, as if she did not want to say any more, she went on gaily cleaning the furniture of her little office and whisking away the tokens from the table with her duster.

XXI

'Do you know that I admire you, Mother?'

'Why?' asked the sister, surprised at Barnier's tense tone of voice that day.

'I admire you and I congratulate you because you can find reasons for faith and causes for hope here, in a hospital ward. I wish I could be like you, I wish it could make me believe in something, to see suffering, death ... but there must be something wrong in my make-up: it has the opposite effect on me.'

'You're in a bad mood today, Monsieur Barnier, I can see that.'

'Now, honestly, do you never have any doubts when you look at this line of beds, when you think of what lies under the sheets? It makes you think of Providence, this hospital, Mother? To die, all right ... If it were only death! But why suffering? why illness? Ah! you know, there are days when my thoughts are in revolt ... You find a Father to give thanks to, after all this? To me, he who poisons the life he has given, he who tortures the body he has lent, he who has made it necessary for people like us to give drugs and to carve people up, yes, the God the hospital shows me, is a deaf, merciless God, a God of bronze and blood like the Christ hanging here.'

'Monsieur Barnier, I took my vows last Monday,' the sister said, in a tone of voice which silenced the houseman.

XXII

◆

'Ah! Mother, it's not next door, the rue de la Bienfaisance. I crossed a little square first: there were dresses drying between two trees, on a clothes-line, it looked like Bluebeard's seven wives . . . Your protégée . . . Ah! that's genuine Paris destitution! Instead of sheets and blankets, she had a heap of wood-shavings! That's where she was confined.'

'My goodness! Is that possible? Wood shavings!'

'But nevertheless at the foot of the bed – if you could call it a bed – there was a fine child, as strong as anything, and screaming with a vengeance. I examined her. It's nothing serious: overheating of the breast, that's all. I've just told her mother, as I walked through the ward.'

'Ah! you were right. The poor woman was so worried. She wouldn't keep quiet. Now, you know, I won't let you off so easily: you'll have to visit the husband of my Number 12, do you hear? You won't be paid any more than for today's woman. But I'm in charge of your remuneration. Every time you make a house call in the family of one of my patients, I'll say a prayer for you, a really good prayer. That's worth at least forty sous, a prayer from me, isn't it, Monsieur Barnier?'

XXIII

In September, Barnier had a holiday. When he came back:

'Well?' the sister said cheerfully as she saw him again, 'That was a real holiday, I hope! Oh! but you've put on weight . . . and what a complexion! You had a good time?'

'Yes, I certainly did. I went shooting like mad. The kid carried my game bag. It didn't give him a stiff back. He's growing up, that brat. He comes up to here now. My mother will bring him next winter to spend a few days. You'll see what open air does for you. I think it stinks here. Oh! it's like sailors going back to sea. It will take me a few days . . .'

'And that's all you did for a whole month?'

'Well . . . I went to a wedding, the wedding of a cousin of mine. Some wedding! It took place in a little wood owned by the father-in-law. We danced for a week. We'd arrive in the morning and leave in the evening. It lasted as long as there was anything to drink and to eat. On the last day we made a bonfire with the empty casks.'

'Didn't it make you want to get married?'

'Me? Ah! that will be the day!'

'Oh! You will get married. It will come naturally, you see. It must be so good, when you've spent the whole day seeing ugly things, people who suffer, all that doctors see, to find when you go home something which takes it all out of your mind, a place of your own, a wife by the fireside waiting for you. You must need them, all those home comforts, when you return from seeing patients. And children! That will be right for you. Noisy children who are asked at bedtime to pray for your patients . . .'

XXIV

One morning, the sister was missing. She was away from Saint-Theresa ward for a few days. For nearly a month she had been complaining of unbearable headaches. When she returned she was pale, as after a blood-letting; she started work again with her old keenness, always lively and quick; she seemed to have fully recovered her former good health.

XXV

It was New Year's Eve. The sister, in the half-joking, half-serious tone of voice of an elder sister lecturing a twenty-year-old boy, said to the houseman:

'You were very smart yesterday when you went off duty at five o'clock. And in a great hurry.'

'I was dining in town.'

'You don't look so good this morning. Are you ill?'

'Not at all, no . . . I came home late.'

'You were out all night, I suppose?'

'Oh! All night . . . that is to say . . .'

'It's Monsieur Malivoire who leads you astray, I'm sure.'

'Malivoire? Ah! poor chap!'

'But what on earth do you do for a whole night? My goodness, when one can sleep . . . It's so good . . . Every night I'm on duty I have to renew my sacrifice. If there was no bell to make me get up, I would sleep all day. That would have been my besetting sin, laziness, if I had been my own mistress. Is it such fun to dance?'

'But I didn't go to a dance . . .'

'Oh! I know what you did, then. You remained smoking in a room where you all smoked. That's very bad for you! And then you played cards, didn't you? And for money, I'm sure. That's very naughty! Instead of going to bed early. But I'm not joking. Your mother would say the same.'

'What is this?' said Barnier, finding the conversation awkward, and kicking a parcel on the floor, underneath the sister's table.

'Please don't kick it ... You're going to break ...' she
hesitated ' ... my New Year gifts! You'd like to know what they
are, wouldn't you? Oh, it's well wrapped up, you won't see
anything ... Come! I won't tease you ... When I was very small,
I was taken to the Enfant-Jésus, one New Year's Day, to visit a
little girl. On all the children's cots, do you know what there were?
I never forgot it ... There were toys and harmless sweets,
jujubes ... It was a princess, we were told, who had sent them all.
And it was lovely! Those pale sick little children were so
happy ... if you had seen them playing in their beds! Well, as
nothing is done here on that day for my patients, all the children
who come visiting tomorrow will get a toy and a cornet of sweets,
as at the Enfant-Jésus. And you will see that the mothers will be
even more pleased than the children!'

XXVI

◆

'There were four of us – me, Dubertrand, Noël and his mistress.
She's very pleasant, Noël's mistress.'

Malivoire, lighting his candle from the gas lamp in the
duty-room, was talking to Barnier who was sitting at the table,
resting his forehead on his hands, his eyes on a medical text-book.

'Oh! it was very merry. The wine waiter looked after us well. You
know, he was here once, in Noël's ward. He brought us some wines
from the cellar – wines indeed! They were as dark as prune juice.'

Malivoire sat down on the table, holding his burning candle.

'Yes,' he repeated, 'she is very pleasant, Noël's mistress . . .'

'Why should I care?' Barnier said.

'Shall I tell you what we had for dinner? Imagine: we get
there . . . no room left . . . They put us in the bedroom of the
owner's wife. At the back, behind the bed, there was her wedding
head-dress under glass. It worried us, that head-dress, staring at us.
We made a salad out of it in the end. Well, it didn't taste good. Ah!
Emma was there too . . . She enquired after you. I say, Barnier,
speaking of Emma, do you know it's amazing?'

'What?'

'We've never known you to have a mistress . . . a real mistress, I
mean . . . call it what you like, a regular girl-friend. You've never
been known to keep a woman longer than twelve hours.'

'Well! Twelve hours with one woman, don't you find that
enough?'

And Barnier, swivelling his chair round and straddling it, went on, stretching out his hand towards a pipe, forgotten on the table:

'Malivoire, I'm sorry for you. You have the wrong ideas about mistresses. Do you know how our elders solved that problem? Better than you. When they'd been working for a whole month, having their meals brought to them in the theatre so as not to waste time, I mean really *working* night and day, what I call work! They even had lice in their boots and didn't notice it! Well, after that, they descended on Paris like wolves, they went somewhere where they could find wine, food and women . . . And it lasted thirty-six hours! Like a sailors' party! They belonged to the old school, the school of Bichat and others. Well-built proud men who didn't drink mineral water. And that's the right school, old man!'

'Well, I maintain . . . I'm going to tell you something silly, but it's true, I maintain that we need even more than other men something more than . . . than lust. Yes . . . it sounds paradoxical if you like, but for us, a woman must be something more. It's all that surrounds a woman . . . the fancy-work, which is made for us. It's the dress, the illusions, all the pretty trimmings. That's what can grab us. Because in our position – our position which is as materialistic as can be, not poetic – we have a great stock of dreams to use up.'

'So, Malivoire, you're platonic, tonight, like a drunk.'

'Not at all. I'm only saying . . .'

'You're talking nonsense!' Barnier said impatiently; and, warming to the subject, he went on: 'If you told me that after what we see we need to love a young, fresh body, a creature bursting with life, healthy from head to foot, a body which makes your eyes forget illness, old age, physical disabilities, a woman who defies death, flesh which makes you want to bite into it like a beautiful piece of fruit, skin from which blood spurts out under a pinprick . . .'

Barnier stopped. He glanced absent-mindedly at the table with the empty bottles, decanters, coarse china coffee cups, saucers filled with soaked cigarette-ends and matches, knives thrown over napkins, a plateful of sugar, seasoned pipes here and there; then, looking up at Malivoire:

'You think I can't love? You think I've never been in love, don't you?'

At that moment, the glazed door of the duty-room opened. A man with a goatee came in, wearing a belted overall. He had the unconcerned, cynical face of a male nurse. Lounging, both hands in his trouser pockets, he said to Barnier:

'It's Number 9 in Saint-Paul ward. You know, the one whose chest you sounded this morning. He says he can't breathe, and he finds it a nuisance.'

XXVII

—◆—

'It's dreadful!' Sister Philomène was telling Barnier, one evening, 'I can't get rid of these migraines. I have one today. I can't see properly. Have you got something for migraine?'

'Not much. Nothing at all. Well, yes, in fact . . . I'll tell you what works quite well for me. Perhaps it will work for you too.'

Barnier asked a ward orderly to bring him a cup of black coffee, and, picking up a laudanum bottle:

'Here you are,' he said, 'fifteen drops of laudanum in a cup of black coffee, that's my medicine.'

'Fifteen drops!' the sister exclaimed, taking fright.

'I could take forty. But all right, I'll only give you ten.' And, counting ten drops from the bottle: 'It's the opposites which, while contending with each other, do . . . Between you and me, I don't know what they do, but they certainly lift off neuralgia like a dream. You'll take a little longer to go to sleep, that's all. Now, drink it and you'll be surprised.'

After one gulp, the sister stopped and said laughingly:

'I hope you'll come tomorrow to find out if I've been poisoned?'

'Tomorrow? Impossible, Mother. I'm off for two days with a friend in the country. He's written to tell me there are wild ducks on his land. You see, I'm not too worried about you.'

XXVIII

After a tiring day, the sister usually fell asleep instantly; she had to fight against sleep to be able to finish her prayers every night.

That evening, her weariness kept her awake in a sort of fever. She spent hours, which she could hear ringing quarter after quarter, tossing under her stifling bedcovers, searching all the time, in her overheated bed, for cool places to stretch her limbs, to rest her cheek. Her half-sleep was interrupted by those sudden jolts which shake the body, right down to the feet, giving the impression of falling. And when she did sleep, she struggled with the strange dreams which torment chaste women.

She found herself in spaces where all was light, but nothing appeared more clearly to her eyes than the patterns of an engraved mirror in which candles sent flashes of lightning. The light looked like glimmers in the clouds. In front of her, large expanses opened up where there seemed to be no living creatures; and yet they were neither sad, nor empty, nor deserted. Life was everywhere, as in a ray of sunshine, blinding and invisible. What she heard was the silence of noon on a beautiful day, the sound of the hushed wind, of the sleeping grass, of the earth at rest, of the birds flying without song, a melody which was only a whisper and a breath. What she breathed was a breeze which scattered the dew, like the sprinkling of a fountain. All sorts of vague, sweet sensations arose from veiled gleams and harmonies, mirages and echoes which softly lulled the floating dreams of her sleeping senses. Losing herself in that vision, she felt a tickling on her neck; it brushed against her like a fly, which, in the morning, flits around and lands on the face of a half-awakened sleeper. In her dream she wanted to flick off with her hand that tickle which, running over her skin, always returned with a troublesome teasing; but soon her slow hand was too lazy to pursue the obstinate tickle. Then it was no longer a fly brushing against her neck; it felt like the wings of a butterfly quivering against her skin, faster and faster. The quivering became a caress. The two wings wandered instead of flying: they were two lips, two lips without any body, without any face, two lips, free and alone in space, which were only one mouth and one kiss, a kiss which started with a ticklish caress on her ear, and became as painful as a love-bite . . .

XXIX

It was half past eight. Morning lazily surfaced after the long February night; the first glimmer of a beautiful winter day was creeping across Saint-Theresa ward. The ancient window panes were turning green against the white sky.

In the middle of the ward, twenty young men, housemen, non-resident and second-year students with portfolios under their arms, were forming a circle around the consultant, a pale old man with white hair hanging down behind his ears and black eyebrows which kept quivering above his small eyes, still lively with youth, deep, soulful and kind. The old man, with a white tie, a black suit, the rosette of the Legion of Honour in his buttonhole, was wearing a large white apron. A garnet-red velvet skullcap, leaving his wide forehead uncovered, rested on his white hair. He was calm, smiling; glancing around him at the young men and absent-mindedly touching the stove-pipe, he seemed to laugh inwardly at a joke which rose to his thin lips. Among the young men around him, some had fastened the corner of a large white apron to their first coat button; others wore cloth hearts studded with pins in their buttonholes; they talked cheerfully, but in a low voice: their laughter was respectful of the place and of the master. However, youth still had its day; one could hear at times a woman's name, some piece of gossip about the previous evening's dance. Separate groups talked to the patients. Two of the younger students, racing, had stopped at a bed in which a patient held her knees clasped against her chin; leaning their elbows on the empty foot of the bed, they were struggling, playfully trying, like young puppies, to push down each other's wrists.

On a long table placed between the two stoves, strips of cloth were rolled up. A pyramid of small sponges stood next to the snowy heap of shredded linen. On a little desk, wooden pigeon-holes were filled with jars of yellow and brown ointment out of which stuck spatula handles. The high flame of a small spirit lamp threw warm golden glints into copper basins. At both ends of the table, silvery lights played over two pewter containers with dull, elongated reflections. A houseman, leaning over the table, was leafing through a register which bore at the top of its columns the headings: *Infusions; Medicines: external, internal; Broths: with rice; with noodles; with fat; with milk; Bread soup: fat, lean; Solid food: 1, 2, 3, 4; Drinks: wine, milk.* Leaning against the table, a thick-set, short-legged ward orderly was rubbing with a cloth a pewter water-jug which shone between her large hands and screwing up her small red-rimmed eyes, one of which, pulled down at the corner, was smaller than the other.

The ward had been aired and had lost its smell, except for a sort of damp heat: the tepid atmosphere of a room with a steaming bath.

In the pale, transparent, cold light, each bed was clearly delineated as a white square, with its cambric muslin surround, its woollen blanket or green eiderdown. Sunbeams seemed to sit at the foot of the beds or, creeping up the sheets, to jump onto the sleeve of a patient who was sitting up. The notices above the beds stood out, stretching to the end of the ward, white when the bed was occupied, black when it was empty. In the bluish light, at the tops of the beds, behind the patients' heads, one could see small shelves bearing jam jars, medicine bottles, oranges, sometimes a book. Between the open curtains hung like plumb-lines the short sticks attached to the rods which the patients grasped to pull themselves up.

Among the reclining women, some looked as if buried in their sheets. Part of a cheek, of a forehead, then a tight round shape, a body folded up on itself, in a heap, was all you could see on the bolster and under the blankets. Others remained motionless on their backs, knees up, raising the blanket at right-angles. Many, their heads high on the pillows, were holding their right wrist with their left hand, attentive, with absent-minded eyes, as if feeling their own pulse. In the beds near the entrance there was some movement; a sort of tidying-up, an attempt at titivating rallied the strength of the least ill. Blue-veined thin hands, shaking a little, were buttoning up the wristband of a nightdress or smoothing out the folds of a bedjacket. One patient was unfastening an embroidered bonnet pinned inside her bed curtains; another was combing her hair.

All were pale, of a paleness which the whiteness of the pillow-cases, sheets and curtains fresh from the wash turned to an ashy complexion. Lying thus, waiting, so pale against that clean linen, their eyes widened by fever, those poor working women showed on their faces and in their bearing the strange, distinguished look which sickness seems to lend to poor men's wives, as if all women, whether ladies of leisure or working girls from the rue de Charenton, had the same grace when suffering.

Over the bed notices, the students had placed their hats; behind the beds, the chairs stood upside-down, legs in the air, to leave the surgeon a free path to the patients.

Standing against a window, her back to the light, her face luminous in the pale shadow of her white veil, Sister Philomène was knitting a stocking.

'Come on, gentlemen,' said the consultant; and, walking down the ward, he went to the first bed on the left of the entrance. He held himself straight, moving his legs stiffly, with a regular dragging step which slithered along the flagstones. The ward orderly followed him, carrying in one hand a towel and a pewter jug, in the other a pewter basin propped against her hip.

Each bed where the surgeon stopped was surrounded by the students, hiding the uncovered patient with their backs, their heads pressing against each other under the curtains.

Silence filled the ward – an expectant, respectful, almost solemn silence. One could hear the squeaking of the houseman's pen on the prescriptions ledger as he wrote, leaning his back against the foot of the bed. All mouths were closed, all suffering was hushed in the path of the surgeon who went from one patient to the next with an impassively gentle face, a confident, encouraging smile, cheerful words and sometimes even good-natured jokes.

'Come on!' he said to a woman whose throat he had operated a few days before. 'You know it's for today. You promised you'd sing us something. Just a little tune, let's hear it . . .'

And he listened to the notes which the patient, cheered and revived, was struggling to produce.

'A helping for Number 9!' the physician said after stopping for a while next to a bed; and the pale young woman who was sitting up in that bed smiled on hearing those words, as if resurrected: life returned to her eager, sunken eyes in a flash of radiant happiness.

The surgeon was by the last bed but one, Number 29.

'Ah! Yesterday's arrival,' he said, looking at the notice at the foot of the bed.

The patient opened her jacket and uncovered her breast. A houseman lifted the bed-curtain to let in the light from the window. The physician looked. The patient was watching his eyes, but those eyes gave nothing away.

After half a minute, the curtain dropped again. The woman closed her eyes, she heard the surgeon turning round, moving away. A sudden wordless terror seemed to lay an icy hand on her back. She buried herself in the bed, pulling up the blankets and hiding her face in the pillow.

'Isn't Monsieur Barnier here?' the physician asked, walking to the next bed and looking at the group of students.

112

'Here he is,' a voice said, 'he's coming.'

The students were surrounding the bed at the head of which the surgeon had stopped. Barnier slipped in behind them, in the space next to the bed which the surgeon had just left. He was standing, waiting for the consultant, who faced him, to speak to him, when he felt a hand grasping his hand from behind; he turned round: suddenly he was afraid, like a man who has seen a ghost from the past.

'What are they going to do to me, Barnier?' asked the patient in the bed, whispering in his ear.

'You!' Barnier said. 'You?'

'What are they going to do to me? Tell me!'

'Monsieur Barnier!' the surgeon called on his way out.

Barnier followed him and, as he was walking down the stairs next to him, the surgeon said:

'Monsieur Barnier, I know that housemen complain about leaving the hospital without having done any operations. Well! I want to try it out. You will operate on the new arrival, Number 29, tomorrow. You saw her: a lardaceous encephaloid on the right breast. I would advise a convex scalpel for cutting the teguments, a straight scalpel for the rest of the operation. And make a curved incision . . .'

XXX

The surgeon was still talking, but Barnier no longer heard him.

He had loved that woman. He had been her first lover. She came from the village where he was born, a tiny village of bargees on the bank of the Marne. Her father was a barge owner who worked at towing with his horses along the Meaux canal. The village with its screen of poplars, the river, the ducks, the horses being washed, the tiled roofs, the main street, her house, her window where, at night, he could see the dark vine-leaves against her lit-up curtain; the first kiss he had stolen, on her neck, just below the hairline; the barn full of hay where the sun stealing in through the trapdoor touched the hem of her skirt; the little wall over which she jumped, when the household was asleep, to go to a dance; and that ravine where they wandered in the summer – how far away it all was, and how near! So long ago, and yet it felt as if it were yesterday.

In Paris, where she had followed him when he came to study medicine, how happy they had been: mad carnivals, picnics when the weather was fine, improvised suppers at the foot of their bed, the pleasure of new dresses for her, jealous fits wiped out by a caress! Until the day when she had left him, when his student room, still full of her presence, had seemed as empty as a still-warm nest from which the birds have flown . . .

All those memories crowded in on his mind, his eyes, all mixed together, in fits and starts.

XXXI

◆

After the consultation in the men's ward, Barnier came back to the patient's bed:

'What did he tell you?' she asked, taking hold of his hands. 'Will you have to use . . . your instruments?'

Barnier felt her shudder through his fingers.

'No . . . no . . .' he stammered. 'Ah! My poor Romaine. You here!'

'Me here . . . Yes, I've run wild, since I last saw you! I've had ups and downs,' she said with a strained smile. 'It wasn't always fun. You see, there are some men, when they've been drinking, they have to break up everything, glasses . . . and women . . . That's what my last lover gave me . . . a blow with his fist. Look . . .'

She showed him her breast.

'Will they cut it off? They won't cut it off, will they?'

At that moment, Sister Philomène came near the bed and said, in a voice Barnier had never heard her use:

'Number 29, you speak too loud, it disturbs your neighbours' rest. And you too need rest, much rest.'

And the sister, coming to the bedside where Barnier was standing and almost pushing him away, started tucking in the bedclothes again, right up to the bolster.

'Mother,' Barnier said, following the sister, who was leaving the bed, 'You really should – you know how to give people courage – I don't know how, I can't do it . . . It's a woman I used to know long ago, and I haven't the strength . . . we have to operate tomorrow. There's only today to prepare her . . .'

'She will have the operation tomorrow?' the sister said, in a strangely cold voice.

Barnier had to repeat: 'Yes, tomorrow. She is afraid – you've seen her – a very nervous temperament. Please, talk to her, prepare her . . . You are so kind. I've often seen you obtain from patients what we physicians could not obtain. Tell her the operation will be easy. Make her accept it, please, Mother? Without frightening her . . .'

After a moment's silence: 'I shall speak to her. And perhaps God will suggest good words to me,' the sister said, turning towards Barnier a face on which he was surprised to see an expression of suffering.

Barnier went back to his room. He spent all day reliving the past history of his love; heady memories arose in his mind, with the wild scent of field flowers and fruits of the forest. All the time, he passionately wanted to go and see Romaine, but he did not dare approach her bed; he was afraid of a word, of a question, and his cowardice won. He thought that the sister would speak to her and he feared she would not succeed, would not persuade her to have the operation. A minute later, he would be sure the sister had succeeded, and then, thinking of the following day, he would tremble all over. He told himself that his place was by Romaine, that he should help the sister to sustain her in her weakness; that he should speak to her, tell her that the operating surgeon would take pity on her beautiful body . . . And he stayed, lacking the courage and allowing his eyes to roam in spite of himself towards the cold steel instruments in his kit.

XXXII

In Saint-Theresa ward, two women were talking from their beds, the embroiderer of petticoats and an old woman whose face was half hidden by a bandage which covered both her eyes.

'I say, you with the embroidery, isn't it nearly four o'clock?'

'Yes, it is. You can see it from the light.'

'You can see . . . it's all right if you can see . . .'

'Ah! I forgot.'

'Why don't we hear Sister Philomène today? She's very strict about the time, usually.'

'Perhaps there's something wrong with her. She didn't look her best this morning. You couldn't see: she didn't call the little girl in Number 5 to give her a treat as she usually does. Ah! here she is. She's with Number 29. The ward orderly told me that they're going to cut something away from her tomorrow, Number 29. That's why. She's working on her, she's telling her to make up her mind. Can you hear? You're nearer.'

'Of course I can hear her . . . It's funny, she isn't using her good voice, you know, her voice . . . when she speaks with that voice you'd do anything she says.'

'Ah well, perhaps there's a hurry and the other one is being awkward. When there is time, they don't rush you. I know, I've seen it so often. They treat you gently. They're cunning, you know! They see at once, you understand, they have a trained eye, if you're one of the *nervy* ones, as they say . . . Then, for two or three days, they tell you that they're not doing anything: "We'll have to see . . . We'll see," words like that. Then you're in suspense. You don't know whether they'll operate: never mind; your mind is working on it, the idea goes round and round your head . . . When they see you like that, they start saying, softly, without insisting: "In your place . . . you see, if I were you . . . you'll do what you like but . . . I'd get rid of that thing." Then they leave you for another day or two to mull over the idea. And then, one morning, they leave off the soft soap and they say bluntly: "My good woman, if you don't have that thing removed, it will be the death of you." That gives you the final blow, and since you've been on tenterhooks for a week, you might as well have done with it. But for her, it's different . . .'

'What does she answer, can you hear? Has she made up her mind?'

'I'm not sure. She doesn't say much. She's mumbling . . . She's talking about her body . . . "My poor body . . ." that's all she says. Ah! the sister is tough with her, my goodness! That's not the way she could convince me, if I didn't feel like it. Is she talking to her about death? Oh God!'

'Well, you know, if they didn't frighten you a little, you would never make up your mind. Ah! it's finished. Here's the sister. Yes, it's true, she does look ill.'

XXXIII

The next day, around eleven o'clock, two nurses brought up a stretcher on which lay a pale woman, looking subdued, as if tamed, with frightened eyes and an anguished expression of shamefaced fear.

The houseman and Sister Philomène, assisted by a maid, put her back on the bed with the utmost care. When Romaine was in bed, her head high on the raised pillow, a sudden exaltation replaced the submissive, fearful, shamed attitude which gives patients, after an operation, the look of children who have just been chastised.

'I love you, Barnier!' she said, and a flood of loving words poured out of her mouth, like a flight of kisses.

Barnier silenced her with a gesture and, having made her promise to be quiet, he hurriedly left the ward, whilst the notice at the foot of the bed was inscribed: *Operated on February 7th.*

He met Malivoire on the stairs.

'Are you coming to have lunch?'

'No,' he answered, 'I'm not hungry this morning.'

Hurrying back to his room, he collapsed into his armchair; just in time: his legs were giving way under him.

The woman's body appeared in front of him and he couldn't escape from it. His eyes saw the small, round, cool breast where his head had once rested; his scalpel was cutting into it, his hand was pressing the steel . . . And the sight of that horrible moment did not end: it started over and over again and he seemed to be operating again and forever!

His apron was stained with blood; he hadn't noticed it. He threw it away from him and went up to Saint-Theresa ward.

Seeing him, Romaine, half opening her large eyes which had rings under them, gave him one of those wordless smiles with which patients ask to be left alone with their suffering, with their thoughts, with silence, with rest.

He came back several times. Romaine always greeted him with that sweet, sleepy, lazy smile.

On his last visit, during the night:

'Barnier,' she said in such a low voice that the houseman had to lean over her to hear it, 'you have seen me, haven't you? You have seen my body afterwards . . . Is it horrible? Is it very large? I shall be a fright . . . It would be better to be dead, wouldn't it? Why did the sister come to speak to me? Who will want me now? Ah! yes, they should have let me die. You used to find me so good looking . . . you used to be proud of me, remember? Now you wouldn't even dare look at the place . . . I tell you, it would have been better to end it all!'

XXXIV

◆

'Why are you fidgeting like this, child? You must keep quiet,' the surgeon said the next morning.

He came near her, looked at her, felt her skin: then, uncovering her chest, he sounded it at length.

'Monsieur Barnier, do you find anything abnormal? With the heart? The lungs?'

'Nothing . . . nothing.'

'That's what I thought. Everything is fine, child.'

Reaching the end of the ward: 'Gentlemen,' said the surgeon to the housemen who were following him, 'I told you there would be no class . . . I have changed my mind. Let's go downstairs.'

And when the housemen and students were ranged around him on the steps of the theatre:

'Gentlemen, I want to talk about patient Number 29. The operation, which I entrusted to one of you, has been carried out perfectly. I could not have done better than Monsieur Barnier. You have just seen that poor woman, you noticed how carefully I auscultated her; I asked Monsieur Barnier to repeat the auscultation, and, as you heard, we found all the organs functioning normally. The operated woman has neither erysipelas nor an abscess, nor any symptoms of peritonitis, pleurisy, pericarditis or abdominal lesion. There is nothing to worry about, and yet, I must tell you, I am very worried. We must admit it, gentlemen, painful as it may be,' the surgeon went on sadly, 'our knowledge, our experience sometimes come across mysteries which defy them and put them to shame, mysteries of which we know nothing, in spite of our studies, of which we see nothing, in spite of our efforts, of which we can only say one word: an accident! Because that is the only word we have to describe the unknown. I once had, five or six years ago, a patient operated on for the same ailment. The day after the operation, I found her worried, anxious, restless, feverish, fidgeting all the time; and, like today's patient, with no internal disorder. She died three days later, and the post-mortem taught me nothing about the cause of her death, revealing no material alteration. Monsieur Barnier, you have been warned. Watch the patient closely. And, you understand, apply the strongest treatment.'

XXXV

◆

'Water! Give me water!' Romaine said to the houseman when he went back to her bedside. 'Ah! I don't feel well . . .'

She kept moving about, fidgeting, turning her head to the left and the right on the pillow, stretching and bending her arms, raising one leg, lowering the other. She complained about choking, about pains in her back, sickness, a general ache all over her body. Barnier spent the whole day and night nursing her, watching over her, fighting the violent sickness with violent remedies: he was unable to tame her restlessness, to bring down her fever, to quench her thirst, to lull into an hour of sleep the twitching of her limbs which kept stirring under the sheets.

In the morning, during his round, the surgeon lifted the dressing. The wound seemed healthy. But the patient was in a state approaching delirium and all hope was lost.

XXXVI

◆

Romaine was refusing to speak to Barnier. Suddenly, during the day, she grasped his hands roughly and angrily, entwining her fingers in his, holding on to him with all her strength and with her glance, with her two large eyes in which the pupils were now only pinpoints in the white.

'I shan't die, shall I, Barnier?' she said in a halting voice, interrupted by choking fits: 'I don't want to die, no, I don't! Dear Barnier, let me live. I'm not old enough . . . You know I was only fifteen then. The priest came, he was here . . . Are you all cheap doctors here, tell me? Oh! I'm holding you tight, you won't get rid of me . . . Well, I don't mind not being beautiful any more . . . let them do what they like to me . . . but let me live . . . only that, to live! To go on living!'

Then, at once, pushing away with horror Barnier's hands which she had held as in a vice:

'Ah! You butcher, how you've worked in there! How you've cut! It's only meat to you, that's all it is! Leave me alone, then! I'm glad I jilted you, now. I wish I'd lived it up even more, you know, had even more fun, deceived even more of you men!' She had a smile, which faded immediately.

'Romaine! Romaine! I beg you . . .' Barnier was saying.

But the dying woman was clinging to him again and working her way up his arms with her groping hands which tried to hold on:

124

'The others? What do I care about the others? Let them all die! I'm young . . . I'm strong . . . I'm not finished . . . We live long in my family . . . I'm tough . . . I've never been ill . . . I used to walk across the bridges, in winter, when it was freezing, with hardly anything on, just a shift on my back, on Saturdays when we went to the Opera, you remember? Why is she always lurking about, that bitch of a sister? I won't care a damn about all that when I'm ready to leave. God, how I suffer! I'm so thirsty! Ah! you butcher! If I had had your flesh under my teeth then, you would have felt how I can bite! Yes, water, water, give it to me, my tongue is like wood.'

She drank, her fingers loosened and she sank into the kind of exhausted sleep which seems to be a rehearsal for death.

Barnier was at the end of his strength. He ran away. Under the curtains of a patient's bed, he heard, as he went past, the voice of Sister Philomène saying:

'Yes, it is really horrible. We shouldn't accept those women here. There should be cells. At least they could die without creating a scandal.'

XXXVII

⬥

Dinner was just finishing. In the ward, a last breadcrust cracking under a patient's tooth sounded like the nibbling of a mouse.

Two youngish women in little white caps, white jackets, and black petticoats were walking arm in arm, backwards and forwards between the beds, their mischievous brightness and girlish giggles alternating with the wisecracks of street urchins.

'Sister! Mother!' they said, repeating ironically the names exchanged between the sister and the ward orderlies. 'It's a real family here . . . But they never say "my son".'

They laughed, and one of them, who was dragging her leg, said to the other:

'Not so fast . . . my thigh is hurting.'

Then a slow, plaintive whisper rose from a bed:

'For some . . . it's a leg . . . for others . . . an arm . . . for others . . . everybody is in pain here.'

A scream came from another bed.

'She's yelling her head off,' said the two walking girls.

'Oh! she's soft!' another patient said from her bed. 'She just doesn't care. She wouldn't scream like this in front of the doctor!'

'Well! If I scream like that tomorrow . . .' said a not quite steady voice.

'Tomorrow?' a subdued voice continued, 'I would very much like it to be tomorrow, to know what they're going to do to me.'

'Me too. I would give a lot for the night to be over.'

'It's horrible to see somebody die like this, under your very nose,' said the patient on the right of bed Number 29, turning round. 'She's been gathering up her sheets for an hour now.'

'Madam is packing her bags?' said the two girls, walking past.

The day was fading and going out. The first evening mists were creeping into the ward. A dying, bleak light, like a glimmer of moonlight, seemed a vapour driven up to the top of the hangings and of the beds by the shadows rising from the floor. The cloudy, opaque windows only showed a patch of light on their upper panes and, right at the top, against the curtain rod, a last reflection on the first fold of the drawn curtains. The darkness had already reached most of the ward; but at the back, where the sister's glazed office looked through to an open window, a remnant of light filtering through the muslin curtains produced a sort of mist, like that which rises, at first dawn, from frosty meadows. Against that mist, people coming and going stood out vaguely, blurred like shadows.

The small pulleys from which were suspended the nightlights revolved and squeaked; the lights were brought down, one after the other, within reach of the ward orderly who lit them.

Then, from one end of the dark, gloomy room where the glimmer of the furthest nightlight trembled between four pillars, in front of a small altar, the darkness began to stir, filling with moving shapes. There was a sort of confused crowding, swelled gradually by more black and white silhouettes, but the footsteps of those bodies which assembled, the rustle of those dresses in close contact, made no more noise than crawling worms.

Reaching the circle of light under the hanging lamp, painfully carrying their chairs, the patients arrived; there was a tall, dark woman, her stringy neck wrapped up in a little black shawl tied up at the back, who walked with her arms in front of her, as if she was afraid of falling; arm in arm, two little old women took short steps, bent forward, one supporting the chair carried by the other; a tall young woman with a coil of black hair slightly loosened on her neck walked alone, smart and willowy in the grey hospital coat; then came the two laughing girls, then a woman with a Madras handkerchief and her arm in a sling tied to her white jacket; then a country woman with her peasant cap. Half-carried by two women who supported her under each elbow, a pretty young woman staggered painfully, her head thrown back, with a charming and at the same time sorrowful smile at her two companions who said, when she seemed to flag:

'Come on! Walk, Miss Groggy!'

Sister Philomène, standing on the altar step, was slowly lighting the eight candles of the two candelabra, making hushing noises without turning round when the chattering of the patients grew too loud behind her. As the flame rose from the candelabra, there emerged, shining, the white Virgin with her blue moiré necklace, the paper hydrangeas in their bronze-coloured wooden vases, and the wax baby Jesus in the small crib with the pointed roof topped by a cross. The burning candles cast a light next to the altar on the top of a large cupboard where crutches and deal sticks had been stowed away.

The patients formed a circle with their chairs. The weak young woman had been given the only armchair. Her two companions slipped a pillow behind her back and covered her legs with an eiderdown.

The sister went to the small bell on the wall. She rang once, waited for silence, rang a second time, said in a clear voice: 'Time for prayers!' and sank to her knees on the flagstones in the middle of the circle, facing the altar.

Her voice rose in the silence. It soared under the vault with a piercing resonance, on a sweetly sharp tone, like a cantilena. It was a shrill and rhythmical voice, pure as crystal, thin and clear as a child's recitation, virginal as birdsong; a voice like the soul of an instrument, which seemed to pour out its prayer.

The sister began by thanking God for all the benefits we have received from Him, for having created us out of nothingness, for showering us every day with infinite blessings; and, putting in her own mouth the thanksgiving of the hospital ward, she spoke in the name of illness, of fever, of suffering, saying: '*Alas! my Lord, what can I do in gratitude for such kindness? Join me, blessed Spirits, in praising the God of mercy who never ceases to do good to the most unworthy and ungrateful of His creatures . . .* ' And, from the back of the ward, the stifled mumblings of the very ill mixed with her voice.

A scream, on hearing those voices, rose from Romaine's bed, and words, struggling with confused blasphemies, broke in upon the prayer.

'*Let us consider our offences,*' the sister continued in the same voice, '*consider our offences towards God, towards others, towards ourselves.*'

She was silent for a minute, then continued, her voice ever steady, ever serene: '*I stand before you, my Lord, covered in shame . . . Yes, my Lord, I have been guilty of malice and ungratefulness . . .* '

'The priest! The priest! There . . . shake the curtains!' Romaine shouted. 'Listen! It's their mass . . . they're singing . . . Ah! it's so stupid, that church . . . They left the door wide open . . . Barnier! They're coming up . . . they're here! Ah! the death doctor . . . Go away, you religious maniac!'

'*Let us pray . . .* ' the sister said, in a tone of authority and stern determination. '*Our Father which art in heaven, hallowed be Thy name . . .* '

And the patients responded from their chairs or their beds with a humming drone, at the end of which fell, one by one, from the mouths of the weakest, their delayed '*Amen.*'

'No music! It's a bore . . . Take those flowers away, they stink . . . They can't sing . . . I tell you, I know a better one . . . Wait, it's that tune . . . a funny tune . . .' and Romaine sang:

'Little Katie
Wanted to see the world
. . . .
She got to the tollgate
When an official stopped her
Saying: "You tell me Kate,
I know you are a smuggler.
Come closer my beauty
Come closer still and show me . . .'

'*Hail, Mary full of Grace* . . .' the sister said in a voice which grew higher, stronger, more powerful, and she made the last words of the *Ave* ring out ruthlessly: '*Pray for us sinners, now and in the hour of our death.*'

'Let's run away!' Romaine shouted. 'I'll jump over the little wall . . . Oh! he loved me so much . . . yes, they say his mother had loved too . . .'

'*I believe in God, I make confession to God* . . .' the sister was saying; and her voice, without a quiver, without feeling, commanded silence: it was like an iron hand covering an agonised mouth and silencing delirium on the lips of Death. '*Lord, have mercy on us! Christ, have mercy on us! . . .*' and she went on dropping the versicles harshly, throwing over that woman the litanies of the Heart of Jesus, shovelful after shovelful, like earth to choke her.

'Barnier!' Romaine called, in a broken voice which sounded like a moan, 'I want . . . my hair and my teeth . . . with me . . . I don't want . . . the theatre assistants . . .'

The sister was saying: '*Remember, oh Holy Mary, that it has never been said that any of those who, with their whole trust, appealed for your protection and your powerful assistance have ever been forsaken* . . .'

And her voice had lost its pitiless tone; she did not seem to curse or condemn any more: the gentleness of a woman's voice, the

130

tenderness of an invocation were gradually returning, from one word to the next.

'Underneath ...' Romaine was saying in a dying voice, 'yes, underneath my shifts ... look ... it's there ... my prayer-book ... there, hidden away ... do look for it ... it's underneath ... No! no ... no book ... leave it ... no, no, no!'

'*Our Lady of the sick! have mercy on us!*' the sister said, and her awakened compassion was beginning to throb in her helpless, trembling voice. Now and then her memory faltered and hesitated over the words.

'No ... no ...' Romaine repeated, in a dream. And what she meant to say died out in her mouth under the soothing voice of the sister beginning again, for the *Novena*, the *Pater*, the *Ave*, the *Credo*, the *Confiteor* with such sweet tenderness, such moving gentleness, such caressing pity that it sounded like a guardian angel rocking a deathbed to sleep.

Suddenly, a horrible scream: 'Help! Reverend Mother!' called the sister to Romaine's bed. She knelt down and remained praying until she felt, in her hands clasped by the dying woman, the dead hands growing cold.

XXXVIII

—◆—

Barnier had not been seen since leaving the hospital the previous day.

In the morning, he returned. His trousers were dirtied up to the knees with wet earth and red mud from the fields. Nobody ever found out where he had been during that night.

He rushed up the stairs to Saint-Theresa ward and walked in without realising where he was going. The curtains of Romaine's bed were drawn, and the notice had been removed. His hand groped for support and, finding one end of the large table, he sat on it, with one leg dangling. Behind him, a noise grew louder, footsteps, the rhythmic pace of men carrying something. A terrified whisper ran from bed to bed: *The chocolate box! The chocolate box!* And two male nurses bearing a covered stretcher brushed past him.

The men put the stretcher down at the foot of the bed. They removed and placed next to it on the floor the rounded top covered in brown oil-cloth with a woven cane pattern. The bed-hangings slid along the rods. On the bed, a long shape was stretched out, wrapped in a large sheet knotted at top and bottom like a tablecloth. One man grasped the top knot, the other the bottom knot, and they walked to the stretcher: lifted up at both ends, the contents of the sheet slithered to the middle, sagging horribly.

The lid fell back with a hollow sound, and the two men, breathing heavily after their strenuous work, walked away, whistling with relief. Their steps, weighed down by the heavy load, grew fainter, more distant, died away.

Barnier remained motionless. He was still staring at the same place with unseeing eyes. the empty bed was revealed. Two curtains, thrown over the bedhead, were hanging down at the sides. The blanket, pushed back over the iron bar at the foot of the bed, trailed down to the floor without a fold. A pillow and a heap of sheets lay on the ground. Above the rough brown cover of the metal springs, above the harsh blue of a thin, flattened mattress, there was another mattress, faded and worn out by laundering, almost bleached: the sun, striking it sideways, showed on it the hollow left by a body.

XXXIX

That night there was a great commotion in the duty-room, where the housemen were giving a dinner for the non-resident students. They were arguing over their coffee and everybody was shouting through pipe-smoke. As the brandy bottle, passing from hand to hand to lace the coffee, went over Barnier's head, Barnier, who normally never used it, grabbed it and half filled his empty cup.

'Sisters? Sisters, after all,' a sharp little voice was saying at the other end of the table, 'I tell you, I had a mistress who gave birth in hospital. Well, they never changed her, they let her rot in her underwear! Just because she wasn't a married woman. That's how they are, with their charity! And you only have to see in a ward the different way they treat patients who go to confession and the others. All right, they do good works, but they're overestimated, sisters. Good heavens, there are male nurses and ward orderlies who are just as good, and nobody ever mentions them.'

'Oh! Oh!' exclaimed four or five voices.

'Come on, say it at once, don't mince your words: the sister of charity is a joke! That's what you mean,' said Barnier.

He laid down his pipe on his saucer and went on.

'Look, you're talking nonsense. It's stupid, making fun of those women, and doing it here. Don't we know them as well as you do? Don't we see them at work? Have you seen any here who let a woman rot, as you say, because she has no marriage certificate? Ah! here's the great accusation: they bother the patients with their

134

God. Firstly, they don't bother them all that much, as we all know. And so what? If they bring a little paradise into a hospital ward . . . What would you like to bring instead? Comparative philosophy? Of course, I've read Voltaire too, I'm no bigot, but I find it stupid to bring personal opinions into these matters. My God! Here are women who give up everything, who live night and day in a hospital, who work like labourers, who grow old among all those horrors! Women who spend their lives comforting dying patients, embracing death, without having the support we have: an outside life, the love of science, promotion, ambition for a title or a fortune, a career on front of us. Ah! Good grief! You don't find that beautiful enough? But bring anyone in from the street, if you like, and show him a sister in a hospital ward doing what they all do, putting her hands in rotting sores . . . he will take off his hat, because in front of such devotion, my friend, one may try to be tough and refuse to bow, but the heart salutes – if one has a heart.'

'My God, Barnier, you're getting excited!' the thin voice replied. 'Of course, old boy, it's quite obvious why you're getting hot under the collar. That's a personal matter for you. You have your reasons for defending the sisters . . .'

'Reasons? What reasons?' said Barnier, draining in one gulp the brandy in his cup.

'Don't pretend! You know them as well as I do. We're among friends, there's no need to make a mystery of it.'

'When you've finished . . .' said Barnier, resting his chin on his hand.

'Come on! Your word of honour that you haven't been having a romance, for the last year, with the mother in your ward, Sister Philomène.'

Barnier shrugged: 'I thought you were stupid, Pluvinel, but not that stupid, really!'

'Well, maybe you're not hooked yourself, I don't know, but as for the sister . . .'

'Leave me alone!'

'As for the sister, she's smitten. You've turned her head, poor girl. Those women have very idle imaginations . . .'

'Pluvinel,' said Barnier, lifting his empty cup to his lips, 'you're drunk.'

'Why? Because I've seen what everybody has seen . . . the sister hanging round you like a moth drawn to a candle and gazing at you with such eyes . . . well, the usual game of women in that position. You needn't make such a face: I'm telling you things which are public knowledge by now. You're the only one who doesn't mention it. It's the talk of all the orderlies.'

'You are saying . . . the sister?'

Through his drunkenness, the blood rising to his head, Barnier's memory seemed to be filled with a sudden light. All sorts of things he had not noticed, trifles which had escaped his attention during Romaine's illness suddenly revealed their meaning.

'Right! You've got it, now?'

'No,' Barnier answered, picking up the bottle on the table and pouring more brandy into his cup.

'You haven't? You're really discreet, old boy . . . Congratulations.'

'Pluvinel!' Barnier shouted. 'Pluvinel, you've got a nasty character!' And, changing tone, he started laughing, looking at him above his cup which he was emptying with short gulps.

'Gentlemen . . .' a voice began.

'Quiet, over there! Pichenat is going to give us an imitation of a clinic lesson by the famous *organopathic* doctor at the patient's bedside.'

'Gentlemen,' Pichenat was shouting, sitting at the end of the room, next to the empty bed, in the pose of the distinguished doctor by a patient's bedside, 'I am asking the *animists*, the *solidists*, the *vitalists*, the *organicists*, the *iatro-chemists*, the *iatro-mathematicians* and all other *iatros*! Monsieur Bélard, examine the subject . . . A pain in the frontal, or rather the temporal bone, that's what he is complaining about. Well, Monsieur Bélard, have you percussed? But how did you percuss? Come on, percuss again . . . Sit down, gentlemen, have some benches brought forward. Is that how you percuss, sir? But you skip, you have just skipped three centimetres! The patient's spleen is one centimetre wider on all sides. That's where an unknown irradiation starts. One centimetre more on all sides . . . Gentlemen, I am telling you truthfully, I am indispensable, I know it and you see it. If I died tomorrow . . . Percussion without me would be the world without the *psychatom*. Let us invent words, gentlemen, let us invent words: they sound like ideas! And what about the patient who was in that bed last time, the poor man we have unfortunately lost? Why wasn't I told? It's incredible . . . Such an extraordinary case! So unfortunate . . . I wasn't warned for the post-mortem! It's quite unbelievable . . . no consideration for an *organopathic* specialist like me!'

The end of the speech was lost in the general noise. The good healths drunk in each group, the rounds of drinks gradually went to their heads. On the table, where some playing cards had been found, fabulous imaginary sums were being gambled. One non-resident student, whom they had made tipsy in fun, was now, as they said, *well done*. Two very serious housemen were talking in low voices in a corner with such enthusiasm that now and then one could see them taking off their spectacles to wipe the lenses over their knees, against the cloth of their trousers. Another was singing to himself the traditional song of Bicêtre housemen:

> In this Bicêtre where I am bored to death,
> Deprived of pleasures and reduced to a wraith,
> All alone, I oft meditate,
> Upon the old and the edentate . . .

Barnier, sagging slightly, was leaning his elbows on the table. His eyes were throbbing, his mouth had a nervous drunken twitch and he was chewing rather than smoking a cigar stump, whilst drinking out of the cup where he had poured some more brandy.

'You're drinking a lot tonight. What's the matter with you?' Malivoire asked him.

'With me? Nothing . . . I'm thirsty,' Barnier answered curtly; and as he happened to glance at the game, he started staring, without saying a word, at the cards going backwards and forwards, at the gamblers who were winning. Half an hour later, he found himself next to Pluvinel and, as if he had just woken up, said:

'I say, Pluvinel, what you told me . . . you are sure, are you, Pluvinel? It's true, then . . . that the sister has . . . feelings?'

Pluvinel answered with a shrug. Then Barnier, putting his arm round him, pulled him closer and said brokenly:

'It's because . . . you see, I want to ask you, because you must have thought about it . . . you've had affairs longer than we have . . . it shows on your face . . . Well! I want you to tell me . . . if it hasn't happened to you . . . you know, when one has those thoughts . . . which make your desires awaken in your head . . . to think of . . . a nun? A sacred body . . . a blessed habit . . . something unknown which frightens you like a priest's cassock . . . and attracts you like a woman's dress. I've seen pictures in books, of nuns like that, with a man kneeling in front of them . . . I've forgotten where, some stupid book . . . You're like me, aren't you, Pluvinel? The sacrilege of that sort of love is tempting . . . The veil and everything. That's real forbidden fruit!' and Barnier's eyes lit up.

'So what?' said Pluvinel.

'So? It's time to do my rounds . . . and we shall see.' And Barnier stood up.

'Come, Barnier! Stay here. You're drunk, you'd better stay here. You're going to do something silly.'

But Barnier, who had staggered to his feet, was already out of the door. He walked across the yard and up the stairs, and as he entered the first ward he saw Sister Philomène going alone into her office.

He went in behind her: the little room, hot and sticky like an oven, sent a fiery flush to his temples. The sister, with her back to him, was warming an infusion. He grabbed both her arms and brought his lips close to her face; but the sister, with a great struggle, loosened the grip on her wrists and struck him on the face. For a second, he felt like hitting back, then he was frightened of himself. He crossed the ward, went down the stairs and dropped down at the foot of the steps, on the wall which surrounded the patients' exercise yard; grabbing a handful of the snow in which he was sitting, he rubbed his face with it.

When he entered the duty-room, he had sobered up.

'Well?' said Pluvinel.

'Well, the first one here who doesn't talk about Sister Philomène as if he was talking about his own dead mother . . . he'll get my fist in his face.'

XL

The next day, Barnier woke up filled with self-disgust. He was afraid of what would happen; he felt a coward, as one does after acting basely. By the evening, he was surprised that the management had not summoned him. The next day, he waited again; a week went by; there had been no complaint from the sister.

At times, his cheek blushed with remorse again. He had no excuse. He did not love the sister, he had never thought of loving her. Of course, he had pleasure in talking with her. He enjoyed the moments spent in her office, near her, in that soft light, that luminous atmosphere which seemed filled with her sanctity. He had grown accustomed to the sister's voice, to her eyes, to her looks, to her gestures, to her confiding in him, to her familiar ways. But as he listened to her, as he looked at her, never had a single thought of his gone beyond that white habit which seemed to clothe her in innocence and to enfold the woman's soul within the nun's dedication. In the closest moment of intimate talk, she had never been for him anything but a friend, and he believed he had never been for her more than a good companion. His attempting that violent act had been prompted by despair and by the furious spur of brandy, like a man rushing into danger without hope, almost without wanting to succeed, to evade at all costs a painful obsession.

Then, the thought of the sister faded away. Romaine was in his thoughts again and he remembered only her. He thought of the first time she had left him; madly trying to forget, he had rushed into brutal pleasures, as though casting out of the window pieces of his own broken heart! When he had seen her again at the hospital, he had felt as if he was meeting, after a journey, a mistress he was expecting and who had forgotten to write to him. Her forsaking him, her lovers, what had happened since they had last embraced, all was forgotten and he only wanted to kiss her. Now she was leaving him again, forever this time! It was all over, she was dead . . . And there was nothing left of her except his memory of her eyes, of her mouth, nothing left except what remains inside the mind of the vanishing shadow of a living being. He wished he could believe in something beyond death, in a meeting behind the tomb, in another life . . .

He went deeper and deeper into that death: it surrounded him, attracted him, drew his thoughts with the fascination of an abyss. Everything inside him and around him seemed to mourn that woman. He felt slowly invaded by all sorts of black, funereal, desolate thoughts which smothered him without his having the strength to push them away. And against her memory, which he summoned all the time and which never left him, he felt so weak that he began to drink, using drunkenness as a barrier against death.

XLI

◆

To get drunk, Barnier turned to absinth. He unavoidably chose the liquor which draws from wormwood tips, angelica roots, *calamus aromaticus* and seeds of the Chinese anise tree a spell similar to that which Asia and Africa obtain from hemp, a magic excitement combining coarse Western drunkenness with the idealised transports of Eastern inebriation. Barnier clung to that almost instant intoxication which flowed up through his body to his brain, to the light, spiritual, winged delirium, which gently carried him away in the arms of madness and daydreams.

He would pour into his glass the absinth, from which rose at once the heady scent of herbs. Over it, drop by drop, he would spill water which misted it, and then stir in small clouds the pearly opal whiteness; he would stop, pick up the decanter again, fill the glass and drink the green liquor like liquid hashish. As he drank, he seemed to awaken from a nightmare. His painful thoughts disappeared as if vanishing into thin air. The dead woman faded away. His memories floated under a pink shroud. He drank and enjoyed the fever in his blood, the electricity spreading inside him and filling him with inner vibrations, with stumbling ideas awakening in his head, with renewed intellectual activity. The intoxication which took hold of him was not, like that of wine, an animal stupor: it was rather a shift of his sense of touch from the surface of his skin to the depths of his being. His mind, his imagination seemed to vanish; what still reached his senses was poeticised and transposed as in a dream. His soul was laughing with indescribable happiness, like an infant laughing at the flowers on its crib. His memory would fasten on a fragment of a sentence and be lulled by it. Gradually, the shape of his ideas started wavering, becoming vaguer, softer, more distant: as though numbers were changing into harmonies. His forehead grew heavy with contented laziness; and Barnier would fall asleep with his eyes open, like a man lying in a ray of sunlight, like a plant in the warmth.

And as he grew intoxicated with that unreal life, as he yearned for its joys, its liberation, its flights, its lazy ecstasies, he would return to reality with a harder jolt. Everyday life was for him an unbearable disenchantment. Ordinary sensations became tasteless. The dullness of reality filled him with boundless boredom. He suffered, under the low grey sky of human existence, as a man would suffer locked up in a cellar on the threshold of which he could see sunlight. And in his boredom, memory would return.

Drinking became his real life, next to which the other life was only a misery, a slavery, a lie, a practical joke; in the end, he even demanded from absinth the strength needed for his work. His intelligence appeared to grow and soar under the stimulus: he felt that his heavy, clogged brain was filling with a subtle kind of gas. His understanding acquired the quickness and clarity of second sight. What he had searched for in vain, he now discovered at once. The solutions of problems appeared to him; horizons opened up. He found in his mind a sharpness of perception, an openness, a range which he had never known.

And that fever spurred on not only his mind, but also his body. His hand had never been so confident, so delicate, so bold and clever in the small operations and dressings of his ward.

XLII

But habit soon blunted his enjoyment of absinth. His drinking no longer spared him sorrow and boredom. He no longer felt transported outside himself into a world of sensations which renewed his being. He only felt a warm flush rising to his head, a momentary excitement which immediately disappeared, leaving him to his life like the waves casting a body on the shore.

He had to increase his ration of poison. Every day he drank a little more. He doubled, trebled the dose, taking it up to an amount which should have killed him on the spot, drinking almost unadulterated alcohol. And every day he sank deeper into the artificial bliss where he could enjoy the dulling of all his senses, the silencing of his heart. He no longer expected nor obtained from his drinking the excitement which had seduced him at first, but only the happy, lazy numbness which had come at the end of his first drinking bouts. He sank, ever more sweetly and voluptuously, into a weakening torpor which seemed to loosen one by one all his sensual delights, into an ecstasy soothed by the shadows of teeming ideas and images, into a swaying, like that of a hammock, which rocked his thoughts in a delicious emptiness.

Since he drank so much, he stopped eating. Hunger no longer signalled mealtimes. His stomach seemed to reject everything except the burning liquid. His colleagues saw him, in the duty-room, slowly cutting the meat on his plate, pushing it around with his fork, and leaving it there. At first, they had tried to tease him about it: but Barnier answered with such violence and sharp brutal words that the whole table left him alone and hardly spoke to him. But he did not grow thin; rather, he put on weight and acquired the puffed-up look of overindulgence. Malivoire noticed that he usually kept his thumb bent under his fingers; he was frightened to see, among the symptoms of drink, that sign of death which he had noticed on so many dying patients.

XLIII

❖

'Are you trying to kill yourself?' Malivoire said to Barnier, who was pouring out his sixth glass of absinth.

'Kill myself? Kill myself?' Barnier shrugged scornfully as an answer.

Malivoire, Barnier's friend, was a small young man who concealed a soul of ice under southern gesticulations and a lively speech with a slight Gascony accent. Nothing amused him, nothing entertained him, nothing attracted him, nothing annoyed him, nothing bored him. Passions, pleasures, ambition skimmed over him without touching him. A strange nature, blowing hot and cold. He was always ready for anything: going to a dance if you wanted to go to a dance; going to bed if you no longer wanted to go to a dance; having an orgy if you were tempted to have an orgy; working if you preferred work; fighting if you wanted to fight; as indifferent to this as to that, without his will having the energy to choose, to yearn, to want.

However, he was no fool. He even had some clownish wit. But he was essentially, professionally, uncommitted. Attracted by Barnier's personality, he had attached himself to him, following him like his shadow. That friendship, the only feeling of Malivoire's which was not superficial, his only devotion, had caused his colleagues to give him a nickname based on hospital slang; he was called Barnier's *roupiou* – the name given to students attached to a consultant and authorised by him to wear a white apron and help the houseman with his dressings.

146

Barnier, on the contrary, with his apparent coldness, his thoughtful, intense, almost intimidating face, had the sort of passionate temperament of which casual observers are unaware and which is betrayed outwardly only by fiery eyes and a mobile mouth. He had a nervous and bilious constitution, in which intelligence combined with action and will-power. His spirit came from himself alone, borrowed nothing from others and did not submit to them. He had the moral courage, the stubborn awareness of his own ideas which made him revolt openly against received ideas imposed by one's surroundings, by early education, by everything which constricts thought. Intolerant of whatever looked to him like lies or hypocrisy, he hated Malivoire's scientific sentimentality and grew really angry with his friend's habit, borrowed from the new medical school, of hiding the frightening aspect of diseases under sweet-sounding euphemisms.

Malivoire, used to bowing to his friend's strong, wilful, expansive personality, dominated by a man he sensed ready to carry through to the end his ideas and his resolutions, could do nothing to remove from Barnier's hands the glass with which he stupefied himself. He attempted it, none the less; he tried to stop him with threats, with entreaties; Barnier let him talk, shrugged – and went on drinking.

XLIV

◆

For a time, however, Barnier held back on that slippery slope.

In the midst of his grief and despair, Barnier was still proud of his mind: ambition, surviving everything else, still lived inside him, like a last heartbeat in a lifeless body. He wanted to win the gold medal of the medical entrance examination – that supreme prize which is the hope and dream of all housemen. He failed one exam; there were complaints at the hospital about his carelessness. He understood that the medal which, until now, according to his colleagues, he had been entitled to expect, was going to slip away from him. The bitterness of it brought him to his senses. He retired within himself, he examined himself and was frightened at what he saw. He found his intelligence heavy and sleepy, his understanding, first quickened by drink, now lazy, slow, almost extinct and working only after an exhausting effort. His memory failed him: to recover it, to force it to retain something for a few days, he needed to exert all his will-power. In his conversations with his friends, he was surprised, astonished, alarmed – he with such a precise, concrete, syllogistic mind – by his own disorder, his lack of logic, his woolly, distraught reasoning which was neither logical nor efficient. He listened to himself talking: his words no longer had the sound of clear thinking; the crowding of images, the flow of sensations which poured over him no longer gave him time to cast words into the mould of a sentence, into syntactic formulas; they spurted out in nouns no longer linked by verbs. His diffuse, scattered ideas no longer held together; the thread of reasoning broke in his head. He still came out with an occasional witty reply; but the bond of meaning no longer linked what he was saying to what he had just said. He hesitated, he stopped in the middle of a sentence, of a story, like a pianist finding a note missing on the keyboard.

In the course of that self-exploration, he also found his temper soured, his patience gone, his mood aggressive. He saw himself tormented by irresistible urges to contradict and utter unkind words, with a fierce irritability and a bad faith conjured up by absinth, which gradually cut him off from his friends. He was ashamed not to find in himself any energy or enthusiasm, any courage for action. Indecisiveness about everything, a moral weakness which blunted his indignation and his anger, passive indifference, that was what he found inside himself, instead of a generous, sensitive, individualistic, outspoken personality and sincere, free, vigorous thinking.

Physically, the devastation was even more frightening. Barnier could recognise in himself the symptoms he had seen described in books: the lessening of muscular control, the weakness of the legs, sometimes, in the mornings, a slight peristaltic trembling of the tongue . . .

Then, grabbed by the horrible fear of young medical students whose imagination goes to work on the diseases they are studying and who search their own bodies for frightening symptoms, Barnier, growing pale, looked into his own illness. Turning at once to the most terrifying examples provided by science, he visualised the ghastly punishment inflicted on alcoholics: dying with blood which has already curdled for three months inside the arteries! He thought of those corpses which only leave grave-mould half the work!

XLV

◆

Then there was a struggle inside him between will and habit. He fought with his addiction and tried to tear himself away from it. He went through the anguish, the conflicts, the supreme efforts, the painful victories, the desperate capitulations which finally destroy a character and shake a man with so many jolts that he is left hesitating, disarmed in front of his temptations, longing for final rest. The uncertainty of the struggle soured his temper. His mood became even more sombre. The bitterness inside him poured out of his mouth in ironic words concealing his desolate feelings. On the days when he refused to drink, when his will triumphed, his broken life, his wasted career, his lost health, his weakened reason, a future which he dared not envisage – all appeared to him and overwhelmed him. On those days, the thought of Romaine grew closer and he felt her shadow near him, like a woman waiting in a half-open doorway.

He tried to wear himself out physically, to escape from such temptations and visions; he walked the streets of Paris for hours, across districts he did not see, through crowds he elbowed aside blindly, on and on, straight ahead until the pavement came to an end; and when he returned to the duty-room for dinner, his tired face seemed to have aged by a whole year in one day.

XLVI

◆

One day when Malivoire was standing in for Barnier in his ward, he was struck by Sister Philomène's thin, pale look, and could not help telling her that he found her much altered.

'What do you expect?' the sister answered. 'Everybody changes. I am less altered than Monsieur Barnier. They say that he is killing himself with drink. Has he no friends, then?'

XLVII

◆

The sister was indeed much altered too. In her thin face, her large eyes had the sickly smile of an invalid. Her good temper no longer showed in her looks. Her smile was no longer lively, and when she made an effort to be herself again, when, by a patient's bedside, she managed to be cheerful, she felt, after a few minutes, her false gaiety deserting her. She no longer had the strength to share the trust and hope which she used to give to the whole ward with such lavishness and ease. She no longer felt in her legs the strength which used to take her flying from one bed to the next.

But she had never spent more time with the patients; she had never worked more, walked more, tiring out her body and her zeal in excessive dedication. Her days, her nights, her life were one continuous sacrifice; it seemed as though she wanted to take the execution of her duties to the utter limit of her courage as she looked for the hardest, the most disgusting, the most humiliating tasks, eager to undergo all the ordeals afforded by a hospital.

When, the night before Romaine's arrival at the hospital, Sister Philomène had woken from her sensuous dream, her body still quivering from its effects, she had knelt down in her cell, in her nightgown, and, until the four o'clock bell, she had remained praying on the flagstones, overcome by feelings of fear, of painful anguish, deeply troubled without knowing why, without her naïve and ingenuous heart opening to the thought of love.

She had spent the whole day examining herself, interrogating her conscience. As she delved within herself, she had been struck by the resemblance of what she had believed, and still believed, to be a permissible affection, an innocent friendship, to love – or at least to the idea of love she had gathered from the little she had read in books. Looking back, she traced her memories from the day when, for the first time, Barnier had sat next to her in her office, on that chair. She remembered the pleasure she took in those little talks in which she forgot herself so willingly and which made her find time so short. She had admitted the secret joy, the deep, intimate joy she felt when he praised her, the excitement, the fervour his praise had given to her charity, to her dedication. Searching deeply inside herself, examining the various pleasant or unpleasant soul stirrings she had felt at various times because of Barnier's words, which should have had no effect on her, she remained frightened by all the resolutions, bitter feelings, joys and desires awoken by them; frightened by the imprint they had left on her and the long time they had remained silently in her mind, in her heart. Recalling those moments, she had relived her past feelings: her grief when she had thought she would leave the ward, her trouble while she was waiting for the decision, her joy when she had been told she could stay; and she had wondered if it was really only the ward and the patients she had been so sorry to desert, so happy not to leave. She also remembered how happy she had been when Barnier had told her that he had been allowed to stay in the hospital for his third year as a houseman, and the emptiness, the strange emptiness in her life, during his month's holiday. Following through all she had felt, she recalled thousands of details, of small circumstances which she had not noticed at the time. She reproached herself for the indulgence, the tolerance with which she had allowed the houseman to talk about everything, the shyness she felt when contradicting him, the passive, almost complaisant attention with which she had listened to his attacks against religion, the laughter and the jokes with which she had answered impious remarks which, coming from any other lips, would have made her indignant. And confronted with all those signs, all those symptoms of a guilty attachment, opening her eyes to a vague light, but still uncertain, she had resolved to talk to her confessor and to ask to be moved to another ward.

Romaine's arrival in the hospital, the change the sister had felt in herself, the sudden revelation of her love through the torments of jealousy, the superhuman effort she had needed during prayers to smother her hatred under Christian pity and to ask God to have mercy on the dying woman whom Barnier loved; then the scene during which, evading Barnier's kiss, she had felt so much weakness inside herself that she had had to resort to violence: all those flashes of insight had altered her resolution. Ashamed and frightened of herself, hating her weakness and that love which she saw as a sin, she had chosen her own penance. She had not spoken, she had not confided in her confessor; she had not asked to leave the ward; she had forced herself to stay, to repent, to suffer and seek expiation in the very place where she had loved, where she still loved. She had resolved to remain in the daily temptation of that man's presence, so as to have more pain in vanquishing herself, in punishing, every moment and without pity, her senses and her soul through the ceaseless torture of remorse and of her desires. She had wished that love to remain in her heart like a hair-shirt rubbing against the wound.

It was still not enough for her to crucify her heart: she also mortified her flesh with private tortures, hidden under her habit, and with all sorts of scourges which she remembered from devotional stories. Growing paler and thinner every day, she let her health fade away with a secret joy: it was an adornment of her body which she offered to God as a sacrifice.

154

XLVIII

On the days when Barnier attended Saint-Theresa ward, the sister did not shun him; she merely kept him at arm's length by her icy manner. She stood aloof from him as from a stranger. She shied away from anything which would have brought him to her side and avoided any opportunity to exchange remarks not absolutely essential to their work. For several days now, Barnier had been hovering round her, trying to speak to her; but the sister always managed to escape him by never remaining alone, by always putting the presence of an orderly or a patient between the houseman and herself. Finally, at the end of his round, snatching at a moment when she was alone, Barnier succeeded in saying:

'Mother, I humbly beg for your forgiveness . . . And I would like to hear from your own mouth that you have forgiven me.'

The sister listened to that voice, which sounded surprisingly moved. She looked at Barnier with soft, sad eyes. Her mouth opened to speak, but her lips remained sealed. She walked past the houseman, entered her office and closed the door behind her.

XLIX

◆

The same day, around four o'clock, Barnier was leaving, with Malivoire, the Clamart house where he had just performed a dissection. He came out of the little green door and walked down the three steps.

'We'll walk, shall we?' asked Malivoire, puffing at his pipe.

'As you like.'

They started walking along the pavement, beside the low garden wall over which towered the amphitheatre roof with its four glass lanterns run through with pipes. The air was filled with the smell of a tannery. On the left, smoke from a factory chimney was turning white, in the grey sky. At the corner of the rue Fer-à-Moulin:

'I say, Barnier,' Malivoire said, 'do you realise it's the 20th of December today? I'd give a lot to be in your shoes.'

'Why?'

'Why? In ten days you will have completed your four years as a houseman. You'll say goodbye to the hospital, to this dump,' Malivoire was pointing at the black walls of the Piété, along which they were walking. 'You'll start your practice. You're launched, with a bit of luck. Tell me, have you rented a place?'

'No.'

'What! You haven't rented anything? That's ridiculous. Come, I'll have to do it for you, I can see that. I'll look for something in a district, a prosperous business district, near the Bourse, for instance, that's central, and we'll fix it up nicely. Now, what do you need? A small entrance hall, a small waiting room, a surgery . . . Not too high up, because of the patients. The waiting room . . . light wallpaper . . . something cheerful, a settee, armchairs . . . Good grief! I saw a piece of furniture on sale last week at the auctioneer, just what you need! We were saying . . . for the loose covers, a material with pink stripes . . . You can hang some lithographs by Hamon. On the table, a Turkish-type cloth, and some serious books which you can buy as oddments. The patient who comes to consult you, you understand, always feels a bit gloomy. You need a reassuring room. As for the surgery, oh! that's got to be austere! I would advise oak furniture. On the mantelpiece, bronze ornaments by Colas, that's essential, old man! The two ritual illustrations: *Hippocrates refusing gifts from Artaxerxes* and the other one . . . it can't do any harm. I bet if you found an apartment without my help, you'd choose one without two exits . . .'

From the rue Geoffroy-Saint-Hilaire, they had reached the rue Saint-Victor. The houses were closer together, flat and grey, with windows surrounded by dirty plaster. Barnier and Malivoire were walking past cheap restaurants with dirty panes and dark interiors, past greengrocers offering, under low doorways, herrings and apples all mixed up, past caterers displaying an old piece of cooked veal between empty bottles. After a huckster's stall which half obstructed an alleyway came a wine merchant whose iron grating, painted red, revealed heaps of potatoes behind its bars. Then came a kind of secondhand grocer with barrels of mildewed white prunes, a haberdasher's shop cluttered up with the knitwear and thick woollens with which poor people wrap up in winter, a ground-floor window plastered with cheap song-sheets, a hairdresser whose pasty wax dummies had orange cheeks.

Before reaching the Place Maubert, a half-demolished building still showed, against a high wall, the outline of former apartments, with edges of ceilings, floors, landings, the black marks of fireplaces, the wallpapers with greasy stains at head height.

'If a house like this could tell us the sufferings it has witnessed!' muttered Barnier, thinking aloud, his eyes wandering over those six floors of poverty brought to light.

'And your thesis, Barnier?' asked Malivoire. 'It's not easy, what you've chosen, the anastomoses of the upper cervical ganglion.'

'No, I'm no longer doing that. I've changed.'

'And what did you choose, in the end?'

'Death.'

'Oh no!'

'Yes. I'll tell you what I think. I want to prove that natural death, the death of primitive man, the normal end of everything, natural death no longer exists. In our modern life, everybody dies by accident. Life doesn't wear out: it breaks. It's a more or less prolonged suicide.'

'You are still an organicist, I hope?'

'Of course! The soul is a great nuisance in scientific matters.' Barnier pronounced this last sentence in a strange tone.

'Let's take a carriage . . . here's one,' said Barnier, signalling to a cabby going past.

'It's hardly worth it now. What's the matter with you? You're shaking.'

'I have the shivers.'

'Old man, I'm sure it's your cursed absinth causing it. It's a shot in the arm, like gin for the English. No! It's such a shame, you should stop drinking.'

'All right, I promise you. I won't drink any more, Malivoire. But please, don't talk to me . . . I'm in pain . . .' and Barnier huddled up in a corner of the carriage.

When they reached the hospital, Barnier went up to bed.

L

The next morning, the whole hospital knew that Barnier had scratched his hand while dissecting a corpse with a purulent infection, and was now dying in agonising pain.

At four o'clock, when Malivoire, leaving his friend's bedside for a while, came to replace him and do his ward round, he was followed by the sister. She went from bed to bed, clinging obstinately to his side, but without approaching him, without speaking to him, her gaze always resting on him. As he was about to leave the room:

'Well?' she said, in the curt tone with which wives stop the doctor at the door on his last visit.

'Lost . . .' said Malivoire with a gesture. 'Nothing can be done . . . It started on the right ankle, it has worked its way up the leg, the thigh, all the joints . . . And the pain! Poor chap, one can only wish it to end as soon as possible.'

'He won't die tonight?' the sister asked simply.

'Oh no . . . He'll last the night at least. It's the same as with Raguideau, three years ago. He lasted forty-eight hours, Raguideau . . .'

LI

◆

That night, at ten, Sister Philomène walked into the church of Notre-Dame des Victoires.

The lamps were being lowered; the light of the candles was dying under the extinguisher which was carried from one to the other. The priest had just left the sacristy. The sister asked where he lived: it was a few steps away from the church in the rue de la Banque.

The priest was going in when she followed him, pushing open the door he was about to lock.

'Come in, Sister,' he said, opening his wet umbrella, which he spread out on the entrance tiles.

He turned round: she was kneeling.

'Sister, what are you doing?' he said, quite surprised. 'Get up, my daughter . . . This is not the right place . . . Come on. Do get up.'

'You will save him, won't you?' and Philomène grasped the hands which the priest had stretched out towards her to make her stand up. 'And why should you mind if I kneel?'

'Come, come, my daughter, don't get distraught. Only God, you know, can save people. I can only pray.'

'Ah! You can only pray . . .' she said, in a disappointed tone. 'Yes, that's true . . .'

And she looked down again. There was a silence.

'Come, Sister, sit down here. You are calmer now, aren't you? Tell me, what is the matter?'

160

'He is on the point of death,' Philomène said, standing up suddenly. 'He may not last the night . . .' and she started crying. 'He is a young man, twenty-seven years old . . . He has not been near the sacraments, nor in a church, nor prayed to the good Lord since his first communion. He won't hear of it . . . He has forgotten his prayers, Father . . . He wouldn't listen to a priest . . . nor to anybody. And I tell you, it's over, he is dying . . . So I thought of your Archbrotherhood of Notre-Dame des Victoires . . . since it's for unbelievers . . . Oh! we must, we must save him . . .'

'My daughter . . .'

'Perhaps he is dying at this moment. Oh, please, you promise me? You will do at once what is needed, what there is in the book of the Brotherhood, the prayers, everything? They will pray for him at once, won't they?'

'But, my poor child, it's Friday today and the Archbrotherhood only meets on Thursdays.'

'Only on Thursdays! Why? It's too late, Thursday! He will never last till Thursday . . . But we must save him: others have been saved!'

Sister Philomène was staring at the priest with large eyes in which burnt, among her tears, a look of revolt, impatience and command. For one moment, in that room, instead of a nun in front of a priest, there were, face to face, a woman and an old man.

The priest went on:

'All I can do for this young man at the moment, my good daughter, is to apply to him the merit of all the prayers and good works of the Archbrotherhood, and I offer them to the very holy and immaculate heart of Mary to obtain his conversion. I shall pray for him tomorrow during the Holy Sacrifice of the Mass and I shall commend his soul to God on Saturday and Sunday.'

'Oh! I am glad,' said Philomène, who felt tears softly welling up in her eyes again as the priest was speaking. 'I am confident . . . He will be converted, God will have mercy on him . . . Give me your blessing for him . . .'

'But, Sister, I only give blessings from the altar, from the pulpit and in the confessional. There, I am the minister of God. Here . . . here, Sister, I am only a poor man, a miserable sinner.'

'It doesn't matter. You are still the minister of God, and you cannot refuse me, you wouldn't want to . . . he is dying!'

She fell to her knees as she said the last word. The priest blessed her, then said:

'But, Sister, it is nearly eleven, you have almost a whole league to walk, right across Paris, so late!'

'Oh! I am not afraid,' Philomène answered with a smile, 'the good Lord will know why I am in the street. And then, I shall tell my beads as I go along: the Holy Virgin will be with me.'

LII

◆

That same evening, Barnier, breaking a day-long silence, said to Malivoire:

'You will write to my mother . . . You will tell her . . . that it often happens in our job . . .'

'But,' said Malivoire, leaning over the bed, 'you haven't reached that stage, old man. I fully intend to save you.'

'No . . . I chose my case too well, you see, to be able to get out of it. I pulled the wool over your eyes, didn't I, my poor old Malivoire!' He tried to smile. 'You understand, I couldn't kill myself. When one has an old mother and one wants her to live on . . . But accidents . . . that solves everything, an accident . . . You must take all my books, do you hear, and my instrument case, I want you to keep it . . . Why I killed myself? Come closer . . . It's that woman . . . She was the only one in my life. They didn't give her enough chloroform: I told them . . . Ah! the scream she uttered when she woke up . . . before the end! . . . it has never left me, that scream, since then! Never mind,' he went on, after a nervous spasm, 'if I had to do it again, I'd choose a less painful way . . . And then, you know, she died. The thought came to me that I had killed her. I saw her again . . . I saw her again covered in blood . . . And I started drinking . . . I drank because I still loved her . . . That's it . . . that's all, all . . .'

Barnier stopped talking. He spoke again after a long silence, and said to Malivoire:

'Tell my mother to look after the kid.'

Then, after another silence, he blurted out:

'But she might have said a prayer, the sister . . .'

Shortly afterwards, he asked:

'What time is it?'

'Eleven.'

'The clock's always slow . . . I still have . . . I'll last till tomorrow . . .'

He again asked the time a moment later, and, crossing his hands over his chest, he called out in a weak voice: 'Malivoire!' and tried to speak to him. But Malivoire could not hear the words he whispered.

And then the death rattle started, and lasted until dawn.

LIII

◆

A candle lit the room.

It burnt between the four white walls against which stood out the ochre distemper of the door and of the two cupboards along the wall. One of the doorless cupboards revealed books heaped on the shelves; the other one contained an earthenware water-jug. Above the mantelpiece, painted to imitate black marble, a print of the Gorgon hung from the centre of the bare overmantel. In a corner, next to a spot worn out by the rubbing of matches which had scarred the plaster, there was a small gilt-paper mirror, a souvenir from some country outing near Paris. The uncurtained window looked out on a roof and on the night. It was a room like any room in an inn, in a suburb of some large city.

On the iron bed with its white curtains, the sheet lay over a body, pitilessly outlining the rigid shape it covered, from the tips of the feet to the ridge of a sharp profile, moulding it like a wet cloth.

Next to the deal table, in the large straw-bottomed chair, Malivoire was keeping watch, half dozing, not quite asleep.

In the silent room, one could hear only the ticking of the dead man's watch.

Behind the door, something seemed to glide forward; the key turned in the lock: Sister Philomène stood near the bed. Without looking at Malivoire, without seeing him, she knelt down and prayed as marble statues pray: her dress did not move any more than the sheet over the dead body.

After a quarter of an hour she rose, walked away without turning round, and was gone . . .

The next day, woken by the hollow noise of the coffin banging against the narrow staircase, Malivoire, vaguely remembering the night visitor, wondered if it had been a dream. Automatically going to the bedside table, he looked on the marble top for the lock of hair he had cut for Barnier's mother: the lock of hair was no longer there.